THE REBORN HEART

HER HEART REBORN: ONE

PATTI LARSEN

USA TODAY BESTSELLING AUTHOR

Thanks, Kirstin!

ISBN-13: 978-1-998948-57-4

CHAPTER ONE

It's cold in my psychiatrist's office, as it often is, though she never seems to notice. I stare out the window into the late afternoon twilight, snow falling gently past the glass, the streetlights already on. We're too far up to hear the swish of passing car tires in the slush accumulating on the pavement, but I can feel it like a visceral thing, memory wound around anticipation and expectation.

"Asta, dear."

I turn my head and meet her eyes, Dr. Matt's faint accent impossible to trace. I could just ask, but it's always seemed rude. No matter how old I get, how many years pass in her care, she's spoken with that weird lilt that's like she's swallowing her words. As if they're foreign in her mouth and not for the first time I picture her lips in a different shape, trying to figure out what sort of face would make that sound.

She'd be the first one to suggest I have an overactive imagination.

Not to mention being easily distracted by fantasy.

"You've been quiet this whole time," she says. "I'm here for you, but you need to talk to me." I know. I shrug and huddle and try to focus. "How have you been feeling?" Her pen poises over her leather-bound notebook, the dark one that holds the loose, unlined sheets. If I used pages without lines like that my handwriting would be all over the place, a total mess. Hers is precise, crisp but indecipherable to me. Psychiatrist shorthand, no doubt.

"I'm fine," I say in a small voice, hunching inside my sweater, wishing it wouldn't be rude to slide back into my puffer coat. My hands tuck between my crossed legs, the fingertips icy through my jeans. Maybe it's not cold in here. Maybe it *is* just me. The meds I'm on mess with my system in a lot of ways and it could be that.

"You know I don't like that word," Dr. Matt says, her smile as kind as ever. "I thought we promised to stop using it with one another."

Right. "Sorry," I mutter, chin dropping as I exhale through my mouth, fighting the urge to squirm. Not that she makes me uncomfortable, not really. My whole body demands that I stand up and walk. At the very least, fidget. But she'll call me on that, too, so I have to be satisfied with softly scratching the inside of my leg with my right index finger over and over where she can't see.

Rebellion has a sour tang to it that I can't seem to let go of even if it's not good for me.

"Your mother says things have been a little... difficult for you the last week." She looks down at her notes while I clench my jaw and then very carefully relax it.

Mom worries. It's fair and all. I just wish she'd stay out of it.

"I'm restless," I admit as I turn to look out the window again. Dr. Matt keeps the room's light as low as the temperature, so it feels a bit like we're in a cave or a secret place like that, cut off and secluded from the rest of the world. The quiet consumes me sometimes, so much that I feel like I'll scream just to hear my own voice louder than the light tone I use with her. I uncross and then recross my legs the other way, giving my left index finger the chance to do some work this time. The faint *scritch-scritch-scritch* of nail on denim soothes me despite myself. "That's all. Just restless."

Of course, it's more than that. It's always more than that. But I'm tired of talking about it. Of these weekly meetings that end in either more meds or less, new scripts, tweaks and trials. Constant talking about something I can't change.

Trauma I need to just freaking get over already and start living my life. I'm honestly no longer sure that's even possible even if she refuses to give up on me.

"That's a common symptom of an anxious depressive disorder like yours," Dr. Matt says. "Combined with your ADHD and CPTSD, it's natural for you to struggle with such issues." She's always so gentle, so caring. I don't have the right to be angry with her. Sometimes rage flares anyway, maybe because she's never been able to actually help me.

Not her fault, though. Since I'm the one that's broken.

Poor little Asta. Her daddy's dead and no one can help her.

I shake off the whispering in my head and sit up straighter, actually make an effort, if only to pretend that I might at some point make progress. "I know," I say. "It comes and goes, even with the med changes."

She nods, her deep, amber eyes warm. There are times it feels like she sees inside me, that I'll never hide anything from her. It makes me try. In fact, I know it's not true. She's not all-knowing, because I've managed to keep some things from her over the years. Still, she's pretty perceptive and it's not always worth the effort to fight her.

Besides, she's not the enemy. My stupid brain is.

"How is your journaling coming along?" She never fails to show interest in what I'm doing. The last time I was here, I told her I was working on writing my feelings. It was something to say. Before that it was painting. Jewelry making, pottery, yada, yada. I've tried it all. Nothing sticks.

Except.

"Good," I say, frowning at my knees while my hands, now grasping the arms of the upholstered chair

6

across from her, grip tightly enough that I have to slowly and discreetly unwind so she doesn't call me on it. "I'm working on a story."

She nods, doesn't speak, full, dark-painted lips soft, black hair slicked back from her face as always in that perfect bun she wears. Dr. Matt makes my mother envious, and I know why. Elegant, stunningly beautiful and about as put-together as possible, my psychiatrist could be an underwear model.

I guess I should be grateful she chose this instead.

"I'd love to read some of it," she says. "When you're ready to share."

I'm far from that. Honestly, even though it's the first creative thing I've stuck with past a month, it's shit. It's all *shit*.

"Sure," I say. Clear my throat, because I need to ask her about the thing I really want to talk over and I know what she's going to say. It's the same thing she always says. It's been months since I've brought it up, though, so maybe...? Maybe this time she's on my side. "I was thinking," I say. Stop and cough softly again. "That I might feel inspired to write more if I took a little trip." She doesn't react as I rush ahead, blurting the rest, leaning forward as I fight to get it all out. "Just a short something, a weekend. Even a night away." Anything. Change.

She thinks about it before nodding. "Perhaps you're right," she says. And my heart.

Sings.

But she's not done, looking down at her notes again, her long, polished nails the exact color of her lipstick clicking as she folds her hands on her notes. They're filed into what's called coffin shape, broad in the middle, narrowed at the tip. Not quite pointed and creepy, in my opinion. They suit her somehow. "You know my goal for you is to manage your illness." She smiles again. "How's the new job?"

I'd only been working at the small bar down the street from my apartment for a few weeks. But I'm still there. It's the first time I've held down a job in years. "It's going," I say.

"That's great news," she says. "Maybe, if you can continue to manage that responsibility, a small day adventure could be a possibility." She nods. "In a few months."

Months. I sag back into my chair. We both know I'm not going to still have that job in a few months.

"Yeah," I say. "Right. Great." Enthusiasm holds no sway. Lackluster acceptance is all that remains. I'm done. Ready to go. My hour isn't up, but I am.

Used up, fed up. Over it.

"I'm concerned with your restlessness," Dr. Matt says, reaching for her prescription pad. The sight of her pulling it to her fills me with overwhelming dread. I know what it means, hear the words she's about to say whisper in my head before she says them. *I'm going to adjust*—"your medication," she says. Writes something in that firm, crisp script of hers. Tears the page off but doesn't hand it to me.

She never hands it to me.

Instead, she stands and gestures for me to rise, guessing I'm not going to talk anymore. She's not wrong.

I join her, shuffling my feet as I cross the room to the leather-covered and padded door. I wait for her to open it, the brighter, cheerful outer waiting room a different space, soft music an undercurrent cut off from her office by that hateful door.

It's hard not to feel like being in a stifling prison when I'm in there and I can't believe she actually chooses it.

"Caroline." Dr. Matt is hugging Mom as my mother rises from the sofa. Mom hugs her back, her face tense, that brittle smile she wears around me firmly in place.

"How was today, pumpkin?" I hate that nickname. Dad used to tell her not to call me that. It sounds cheap and contrived from her lips. But I don't have the heart to ask her to stop. Not after everything she's done for me since he…

Her attempts at cheerfulness, her forced brightness get to me, though. Sometimes I wish she'd just crumble and admit that this whole situation is what it is, but she refuses to let me see the real her. Even when I'm at my worst and have to stay in care.

"I'm adjusting some of Asta's medications," Dr. Matt says.

Mom twitches. It's the closest she ever comes to truthfulness. "Again. Okay, no problem." She meets my eyes, her hazel ones wider than necessary, the lines around them deep. She's wearing makeup like she always does when we come to my sessions, though her new boyfriend is part of that trend, I know, not just her discomfort with my psychiatrist's beauty. Mom takes the script from Dr. Matt. "We'll stop at the pharmacy on the way home."

I'm twenty-eight years old. I can come to therapy alone. Except they don't trust me to handle my own medications so Mom comes with me. Every single time.

How's that for a life?

I can barely muster the energy to say goodbye.

CHAPTER TWO

The falling snow accumulates on the windshield while I wait for Mom to come back from the pharmacy, the cheerful interior of the small local store feeling like it's a million miles away. I prefer the silence of the car's interior for the moments I have that stillness, temple against the passenger's side window cold and soothing. The flakes clump, though there's not a breath of wind, and for a brief moment I want to unbuckle myself from the seat, fling the door open and run off through the softly descending whiteness. Disappear into the pale and ghostly shroud of it, never to be seen again.

I jerk upright as Mom opens the door, my

momentary crazy thought subsiding. Dr. Matt doesn't like that word either.

Crazy. It still fits, though.

"Got them, no problem," my mother says with that same brittle smile, stowing the bag with the rattling bottle inside forward in the console. Not like she'd give them to me to hold or anything. "We're running behind, pumpkin. Did you want fast food for dinner before you go to work?"

"I'm fine," I say to my window, far-off gaze retreating to the more immediate imprint of my face on the glass. Unlike Dr. Matt, she prefers that response. "Thanks, Mom."

I'm not thankful. But it makes her happy to think I am, so I do my best to fake it.

Her forced chatter is familiar enough that I'm able to tune her out the rest of the way across town. Why she can't just be quiet I have no idea. Okay, one. I think my mother fears me and my brokenness when there's nothing to be said, so she fills that space with the sound of her voice so she doesn't have to be so afraid. Like a little girl talking in the dark so the monster under her bed won't eat her.

Oh, look. There's my overactive imagination again. I'll take it over Mom's incessant words that mean absolutely *nothing*.

I know it's not fair to think about her that way. She parks and waits for me to climb out and close my door before carrying my pills in front of her like a prize, up the outside staircase to our second-floor apartment. The kid below us on the left is supposed to shovel the snow but he's slacking again, as always, likely playing some video game while his own mother yells at him through his noise-canceling headphones. Mrs. Birch, our downstairs neighbor on the right, wouldn't pick up a shovel if her life depended on it.

Whatever. I'll clear them off before I leave for work.

"Are you sure you want to go tonight?" Mom shivers and looks up into the falling fluff that lands on her eyelashes and makes her blink. "I think we're supposed to get a storm."

"I told Clyde I would," I say, hearing Dr. Matt's voice in my head at the same time. *If you can continue to manage that responsibility.* "I want to go." Funny, I realize I do, and not just to fulfill the obligatory proof my psychiatrist requires, the dangling carrot of a moment of freedom from this life that isn't a life. It's kind of fun, if I even know what that means, and I get to be out of the house unsupervised.

"Of course," Mom says, brightening for real as she opens the door. "He'll be happy to hear it." It helps that she's dating the guy who owns the bar I've been working at. In fact, I'm surprised she even mentioned me staying home at all. I wonder if she's aware of how careful she's been to make sure this boyfriend hangs around longer than a few weeks? Since they've been dating over a month now, I guess that's a good sign. I haven't screwed up her relationship yet. There's time for that, though. "Let's get your new pills sorted first, though."

My new pills. I choke at the very thought of taking

something unfamiliar, though by now I've been on pretty much everything at one point or another in various combinations. She and Dr. Matt have been medicating me since I was six, after all. Despite the fact that even the experimental stuff doesn't help in the long run, they still keep dumping chemicals into me, hoping it will fix me.

I've given up hope, but whatever.

Mom kicks off her boots at the door, our small apartment opening right into the tidy kitchen and I mimic her, taking a moment to organize our footwear and coats as she hands me hers. Not that I'm a huge neat freak, but it's the least I can do, considering the fact she's been taking care of me all these years. With no end in sight.

I join her at the counter, both hands fisted in the back pockets of my jeans, stomach in knots as she portions out the little bottle of cheerfully yellow pills into the daily dose container. She got this one for me for my birthday, bedazzled it with my name to hide the MTWTHFSSUN. It's somehow even more offensive than the old, plain one with its attempt at cheer when the contents bring anything but. "Dr. Matt said these are fine to layer with the other three you're taking now," Mom says. "Here you go." She hands me one along with a partially empty bottle of water one of us left on the counter and waits for me to comply.

It's hard to swallow. I do my best not to show it, or the fact that I consider—as I always do—faking it and spitting the new pill out in the bathroom sink. Except she flashes that brittle smile again and I sigh silently before opening my mouth and showing her that it's gone.

For better or worse, we'll have to wait and see. While the restlessness increases, though I do my best to hide it, backing away and heading for my room.

"Asta, pumpkin." I stop at the sound of Mom's voice. Oh, no. Not this again. "If you need to talk…" she swallows audibly while I wait for her to finish. "You know I'm here for you."

"Thanks, Mom," I say, knowing talking to me is the last thing she wants. How do I know? Because the few times I've taken her up on that offer in the past, it hadn't ended up healthy for either of us. "I'm okay."

"I know," she says then, her fake joviality far more painful than any real attack. "Don't let me make you late for work!"

My bedroom door closes softly behind me, not quite shutting completely. Mom made sure to remove the locking mechanism when we first moved in here. She's been doing that since I was small and no matter how many times I beg for privacy, I guess I never earned the right. The first time I'd been sent to a facility for psychosis guaranteed I probably never would.

Because once was never enough.

It only takes a moment to change into my staff t-shirt, Clyde's written across my back over a pair of foaming beer mugs my boss ripped off from the internet to turn into his logo. The smaller version over my heart had cracked already, deep blue cotton faded despite washing in cold water. Well, Clyde wasn't all that concerned about quality, I guess, so it's not something I should worry about.

Mom is on the sofa, watching TV and barely waves to me as I exit. I take a minute to shovel the stairs, though the snow is coming down heavily enough I know it's going to be a big job when I get home. I prop the shovel against the railing at the bottom for when I return and head out down the sidewalk toward the end of the street.

The only reason she doesn't escort me is because it's not far to go. She also has Clyde trained to call her if I don't show up five minutes after I leave the house. The brief flicker of rebellion returns as my boots slip through the soft snow, escape as simple as running off in the other direction.

But to where? And with what money, what means of support? It would only end with cops, losing the job I'm clinging to and more meds. A stint back in care, too, probably. Dr. Matt's disappointment is a palpable threat that's simply not worth it.

I don't mind going to the bar, trading one prison for another. It means I'm out of the apartment, even if Mom's tasked Clyde and his son, Jared to be my jailers there.

Depression always beckons. I'm too tired to fight it.

The bright and tacky neon sign in the window flickers as I pause and look up. White punctuates the black of the sky as snow falls on my face, cold clumps clinging before my skin melts it away. I blink into the moisture and then close my eyes, sinking into the quiet and the muffled chill, my entire being falling still.

I'm wrapped up in the moment, like time itself stands still, embracing me in an endless inhale that feels like a memory.

—a strong hand takes mine, his face through the smoke and flames—

"Asta!" I jerk out of the trigger point, gasping as a familiar voice slams into me, shaking me free of the past.

Jared stares from where he stands in the doorway of the bar, a mix of sullen confusion and something that I can never identify but always makes me nervous on his face. My boss's twenty-two-year-old son's dark eyes look down the moment our gazes meet and he shuffles his feet in the snow on the threshold.

"Coming," I say so he doesn't think I'm a weirdo everyone knows I am.

As the snow sighs around me and the past tries to lure me back.

CHAPTER THREE

Jared holds the door for me, standing a little too close as I pass him, forcing me to turn sideways to make it through the entry. I manage a weak smile for him, averting my eyes as I step inside, shaking the snow from my blonde ponytail. A few local regulars look up and nod to me as I enter, but I just hurry to the swinging door that leads to the kitchen, the scent of spilled beer and cheap cleaner making me want to sneeze.

Clyde is on his phone, one big hand cradling it as he stares down at the screen with a grin. He looks up as I enter, my boss's expression still pleasant on his plain, ordinary face as he turns it toward me. His belly jiggles as he laughs. "Look what your mother just sent," he says in his deep voice.

Cat video, no doubt. She loves those. I watch dutifully and even smile to pretend I'm interested in the kitten singing a funny song as AI moves its mouth before Clyde chuckles again and puts his phone away.

Not before sending her a text, though. "I should probably just close," he says. "Not going to get many tonight, Asta."

"I don't mind," I say, hanging up my coat, boots in the corner, my work sneaker soles traded out, a little sticky as I slide into them. "Really."

He shrugs his big shoulders, tall, broad body that of a linebacker who's seen enough years he's more soft than muscular anymore. But his brown eyes are as kind as ever and he nods, overhead light shining through his thinning hair as I tie on my waist apron.

"I'll let you and Jared decide when to shut 'er down," Clyde says. "I'm going to hang out with Caroline for a bit." The fact that he seems so happy to see my mother should mean something. I blame the meds for not letting me feel exactly what.

"Have a great night," I say, heading out through the door again and immediately start bussing tables, ignoring Jared behind the bar as two of the smattering of customers exit into the snow. I don't mind a slow night, though I prefer a steady one. When it's busy I sometimes get overwhelmed and anxious, and I can't keep up. But when it's slower, that's not always great, either. Too much time to think.

Why can't things ever be easy?

There's not much to clean up so when I deliver the two empties to the bar, Jared hesitates before I grin at him like a normal person is supposed to do. I'm good at faking being okay by now, at least enough to get by.

"I got this," I say. "I know you'd rather be working on other things."

Tending bar is just his way of making his father happy, though he'd never say it out loud. Jared's eyes light up and he smiles back as shyly as always.

"Thanks, Asta," he says, exiting into the back and the little office there. I can call on him if something happens and we suddenly get busy, though I doubt that will be the case. He's free to work on his computer doing whatever it is that he really cares about while I continue my façade of good employee, a girl who has it together and whose meds are working.

Speaking of which, the new pill kicks in right around the time that I've finished refilling one of the bottles on the back bar, a wobbly feeling making me stop and take a breath so I don't drop the heavy glass container. The disorientation passes as a slow lassitude passes over me, though it only lasts a moment as the meds do their thing and level everything out.

I hate the dullness but it's a necessary evil that I've grown accustomed to. And sometimes the peace of not feeling a whole lot is better than the alternative, so who am I to complain? At least whatever this is doesn't strip me down to a wavering inability to function. I blink through the first few moments, grateful the last of the customers don't come looking for refills in the time it takes for me to adapt. When I finally sink into the resulting softness of the medication's embrace, I'm relatively myself despite it.

Maybe Dr. Matt was right after all and this will be the dose that allows me to live a normal life. Or as normal as I'll ever get.

I exhale and spray the bar with cleanser, wiping it carefully, the surface never really clean thanks to scuffs, dents and scratches in the old wood. But it gives me something to focus on and to satisfy my intense attention to detail, part of the reason I think Clyde keeps me around.

That and the fact that he's in love with my mother.

It's not hard to lose track of time and when I look up at the two men who call out to me before waving and leaving, chime of their departure through the door a ranklingly loud sound after the quiet. I realize I fell into a long tunnel of motion and action that's consumed almost twenty minutes. Maybe I shouldn't have come to work after all and my initial hopes for the new mix of chemicals is optimistic. I used to need a day or two to sort out what might happen to me when the changed meds took effect, but that's a great way to lose job after job, so I've learned to cope.

As it is, the silence in the bar is perfect for once, the last of the customers gone. I stop at the window when I move to bus their table, staring out into the snow again, barely able to see the streetlights at the end of the block from the curtain of the heavy fall.

And get lost in it as the brilliant white on black swallows me gently in its peace.

CHAPTER FOUR

The door chimes as someone enters. How much time did I lose staring at the falling white? It doesn't matter, though I'm startled by the sound, hardly a new experience, and am now scrambling to hide the fact. I barely acknowledge the solo customer who's intruded on my mental absence as I hurry to the table I'd meant to clear. I only look up after I've swiped the surface and removed the two glasses, already on my way to the bar.

He's not the usual sort who frequent Clyde's, tall and broad-shouldered, the view from the back as I pass him weirdly familiar. I shake off that odd feeling, noting the snow melting in his dark hair, across the tops of his shoulders, his heavy wool overcoat quickly beaded with moisture as the snow he's tracked in melts. I find I'm staring as I circle the edge of the bar and deposit the empty glasses into the sink, unable to stop as each of his features comes into sharp focus, almost in slow motion. He has a wide, square jaw, shaven smooth, a full mouth and high cheekbones, classically handsome, though I find I'm struggling to settle on an age guess. His black hair curves back from his tall forehead, sweeping aside almost casually though in a perfect wave that frames his face with a softness that might otherwise be missing. Gray eyes watch me from under his dark brows, a faint tilt to his head an inquiry, a question unspoken.

Why does it feel like he doesn't have to ask whatever question that is but I really, really want him to?

"Hi," I blurt, dropping the rag to the counter and trying a smile. It's not fake, surprisingly, and feels like I even have some feeling behind it. That's new and I'm grateful to the new meds for allowing me that.

"Hello," he says in a deep voice. It fires off something inside me that makes me falter and pause. Made worse because he just stands there, staring at me with those gray eyes, not speaking, like he's waiting for something.

For me to answer the question he hasn't asked.

"Quite the night out there," I finally say, the silence unbearable any longer. "You must have really wanted a drink."

He flashes a small smile, teeth very white, but he

seems sad to me now. Or maybe I'm making that up? "I've always loved the snow," he says. And sits suddenly in a smooth and graceful motion, discarding his overcoat on the stool next to him, exposing a fitted dark suit, black shirt open at the throat. I need to stop staring. But there's a fascinating feeling to him, a remarkable echo of something I can't place and I'm grinning—so not like me *at all*—as he settles his big hands in front of him on the bar.

"Me too," I say. "What can I get you?"

"Port," he says. "Please. If you have any."

"Wow," I laugh, a soft thrill of amusement shocking as much as anything else as I go on, "*fancy*." Where is this playfulness coming from? I need to thank Dr. Matt. If this is how her new cocktail is going to make me feel, I'll take it.

All day long *and* be grateful.

"I suppose," he says, equally amused, that sadness I thought I noticed fading. His eyes really are amazing up close, not just gray, I realize, but almost silvery with flecks of gold, too. I've never seen eyes like his before.

Except I have. Where did that come from? And if so, where?

I need to hide the fact that there's a giddiness rising inside me that I can't seem to control. Now I'm panicking that the meds are making me manic. I've had that happen before, the massive upsurge in positivity as overwhelming as the crashes that inevitably follow. I quickly turn and root around under the cabinet behind me, looking for something to satisfy him while I struggle with the anxiety that wants to devour my happy mood.

I need him to stay. More than anything I've ever needed before in my entire life.

There's no need to be afraid because whatever this is I'm feeling doesn't take off like a hot rocket in my head despite my fears. Instead, I'm gleefully retrieving a bottle of port—who knew Clyde would have such a thing?—from the back of the cabinet and standing to spin and present it with a flourish.

"You," I say, "are in luck. However." I eye the dark brown bottle and its faded label, "I do not promise quality."

The gorgeous stranger shrugs, a casual movement beneath the dark suit jacket that makes him look even bigger than he actually is. Some kind of football star? Bodybuilder? He looks like a businessman who's come out the other side of athletics with his physique firmly intact. His smile remains, lighting his eyes, full mouth soft. "I have faith," he says.

What *is* that accent? His English is excellent, but it's not his first language. There's too much of a lilt to his speech, and it's not British, either. Like he learned to speak it a long time ago and held onto the undercurrent of his own dialect at the same time, making it all blend together in one piece.

I recognize it. But how can I? Because I've heard that accent before. I just can't remember where.

Now I'm sure there's something wrong with me because I shouldn't care about such things. The wax seal on the bottle crumbles under my hand and probably for the best because I have no idea how best to open something like this. I vaguely recall watching a video online about fancy tongs and things, but this bottle isn't going to embarrass me.

At least, not in the opening of it. The contents, on the other hand?

The corkscrew doesn't do me dirty either, and I'm gratefully decanting a small amount for him to taste a moment later after the dull pop of the full stopper comes lose in one piece.

"An excellent sign," he says, swirling the sample between his index finger and thumb. I'm staring again, this time at the giant ring he wears so casually, though it's an impressive piece. It looks silvery but it's not, likely platinum, with a large diamond in the center. A dragon coils around it as though protecting the stone. I can't help myself, act without thinking, reaching out to touch his hand, that ring, my fingertips making contact with the heat of his skin—

—heat fires off inside my gut like a coal being lit—

For a moment, I shiver, my touch locked on the back of his hand. When I look up again, his lovely eyes are watching me.

And the coal's warmth *spreads.*

He doesn't say anything when I lean away, a bit dizzy and disoriented. He just swirls one more time before he lifts the glass to his lips. His movements are strangely slow and yet he shows that odd grace again, almost like he's not moving at all.

I really need to sort out my meds.

When he lowers it again, sip satisfied, he nods.

"This will do nicely," he says

My hands are shaking when I fill his drink, but he doesn't seem to notice. Or he's just too polite to comment. Instead, he sits back like we have all the time in the world, the storm outside of no consequence. Nor does he make any mention of the fact I touched him without permission. I should be embarrassed by that lapse. Instead, I'm happy. Where is this feeling coming from? I could stand here behind the bar forever with him sipping port in front of me, everyone else lost in the snow while the two of us just smile at one another.

It's the oddest sensation but I don't fight it. And stop questioning it. For the first time in a long time—if ever—I just let myself be. It's the most marvelous and delicious feeling as the heat inside me continues to spread.

"What's someone like you doing at the end of nowhere and no one in the middle of a snowstorm?" I'm cracking bad jokes like I'm some kind of ordinary girl without a care to be had. Look at me go.

He stills, smile fading. And now he's sad again, I'm sure of it, not imagining it, while he continues to maintain eye contact. It should make me uncomfortable. Shouldn't it? Staring back at a total stranger like that? But his gorgeous eyes just welcome me in like an old friend.

"I made a promise," he says, soft and kind and full of a hurt that has me so drawn in I can barely breathe.

It takes me a moment to realize that's all he's going to say, and another to blurt, "That's a big promise."

He nods. "It was," he says. "To someone I've

27

known for a very long time." He sips before going on and I hang on every motion, every heartbeat, every breath. Why am I only inhaling when he does? Exhaling in the same rhythm he uses? "The kind of promise that can only be put off for so long."

This entire conversation is going in my journal the second I get a chance to write it down. It's surreal and amazing and yet weirdly familiar and I don't want it to end.

"Do tell?" I shrug when he smiles again. "Bartender therapy," I quip, shocking myself all over again. "It's what they pay me the big bucks for."

I'm ridiculous and going to giggle and likely will pay for whatever high this is in short order but for now, I'm here for it. Want it to go on forever.

He leans forward, the glass between his hands, that intense gaze never letting me go. "There was an… unfortunate parting of ways," he says, voice lower than before. I'm leaning in, too, so our faces are barely a foot apart across the bar, my elbows on the wood, chin resting on my hands. It's the first time I catch his scent, some divine cologne that makes me think of the deep forest at night and chocolate on the bitter end of dark and smoke that I want to inhale deeply from him. Drink in like he's drinking that port. "I promised," he goes on, "after a sufficient amount of time had passed, that if she didn't find me as she usually does, I would rekindle our connection myself."

"A woman," I breathe, nodding, understanding even though I have no idea. Love has never been a path I've been offered, not the kind of love I see in his face, in his sad eyes. If only, but who would ever feel that way for someone like me? "She broke your heart, didn't she?"

He laughs, surprise showing on his face, though the sadness is gone just like that and I'm grinning back at him, happy I'm able to relieve him of it, if only for now.

"She did," he says, "through no fault of her own. And not for the first time." He sighs a little, finally looking down into his drink and I instantly miss the connection of our gazes. The heat inside me doesn't dissipate, though, growing stronger as it hums like a living thing in my chest now and I want him to look at me because his stare seems to fan it to life faster.

"If she broke your heart," I say, "why come looking for her again? Sucker for punishment?"

His amusement returns to sorrow, though he's still smiling gently, kindly. "Perhaps," He says. "But she's even better at putting my heart back together."

I sigh. It's a visceral reaction, a soft sound escaping me, like a butterfly emerging from a cocoon as though part of me that longed for freedom finally found it. It surprises me, that sound, as does the moment that follows, our eyes locked, his scent filling me with some strange sense of connection, the heat within burning and burning.

His hand reaches for me this time, his turn to touch without asking, that slow-motion movement of grace and fluidity welcome despite the fact I should pull away. When his skin brushes my cheek, I inhale—

"What about you?" He drops his hand before I get

to lean into his touch and I'm suddenly free from the lure of whatever that was.

Whatever that *is*. It's not gone, not by a long shot. I should be afraid. Anxious. Instead, I'm even more relaxed and happy, so happy.

"What about me?" I offer him more port and he nods, waits for me to refill his glass.

"What keeps you here?" He sips again while I think his question over.

"Sometimes life doesn't give you options," I say.

He nods at that. "And sometimes you have to make your own options."

That idea fills me with absolute joy and I'm grinning again.

"If only," I say, reality trying to remind me that no matter what this interaction might be, it won't last because I'm not that girl. I don't get to have a fairy-tale ending with a man who pursues a promise, chasing an epic love affair. The romantic idea of it is feeding the warmth inside me though and I really have to thank Dr. Matt for the change in meds.

He sits back then, suddenly serious. "I don't know what to do, Anastasia."

Hey, he pronounced my name right. Most people say it like Ana-*stay-ja*. He uses the way I like, Ana-*staa-zia*. I've always preferred it.

Wait. How does he know my name?

"Asta?"

I pull back, jerking away from the handsome and compelling stranger at the bar, staring in startled surprise. Jared stands in the doorway to the back, a faint frown on his face, sullen, worried.

"Hey," I say, fumbling with whatever I was feeling, hating that it's fading, reaching for it again but struggling to rekindle it while the man sips his port and watches me with his remarkable eyes. I need to ask him how he knows my name. It feels like a compulsion, a demand. Who is he? Why is he really here?

But Jared's interruption has shattered the confident optimism, the happy, broken it into two pieces and I'm feeling myself coming down, like the drugs are already wearing off, the high shattered.

I'm in for an epic crash, aren't I? *Damn* it.

"Can I talk to you for a minute?" Jared's voice shakes a little and he holds the door open, as though not willing to take no for an answer.

I don't want to go. I can't leave now. I need to keep this feeling going. It's the most real, the most connected to myself—to anyone—I've felt since... never.

Since *never.*

I swallow and nod because I'm being ridiculous. And I can't argue. Jared will tell his dad and Clyde will tell Mom and Mom will tell Dr. Matt and I'll be in a big mess all over again.

"Excuse me," I mumble to the stranger and hurry toward Jared, passing him on my way into the kitchen. Hating to go.

With a horrible feeling that I've just walked away from something I'll never, ever get back.

CHAPTER FIVE

By the time I turn to face Jared, I'm fuming. It's an unreasonable response to being interrupted and I can't help but blame the medication change, though that's not going to help either of us as I spin and glare at my boss's son.

Jared's unhappy demeanor hasn't shifted. If anything, he's even more sullen, a bitterness in his dark eyes that has me frustrated. It's been obvious to me over the last few weeks since I started working here that he has a crush on me. Why anyone would is beyond me. Then again, the introverted and nerdy young man in front of me probably feels as much like a fish out of the ocean as I do around other people so maybe someone like me seems a safe bet. Whatever his reasons for choosing the crazy chick to pine for, his jealousy is about to meet a boundary he's not going to enjoy.

(While my heart races and a tiny voice in my head whispers, *Who are you and what have you done with Asta Fenimore?*)

"I was serving a *customer*," I snap at him. "The *only* customer in the bar. A *customer* who ordered a *very expensive* drink." I'm shaking. I can't help it. This reaction is new for me, outside my typical careless parameters. Now I'm positive that Dr. Matt won't allow me to continue with this particular drug combination because it's making me irrational and erratic. But I'm in love with the heat inside me, with the coursing warmth that spreads like fire through my chest, my limbs and I'm seizing on this rare feeling of confidence and self-protection that I can't remember experiencing in the recent past.

Hell, *ever.*

"We're closing," Jared mutters, head down, frown an upside-down crescent that ages him. He doesn't go back into the bar or argue with me further, perhaps as surprised as I am that I've stood up for myself, stumbling and herky-jerking his way to the office, slamming the door behind him.

I take a moment to breathe. This trembling isn't frightening as much as it should be. I look down at my hands and let out a soft, startled laugh. When was the last time I noticed details about myself? My nails need a trim and I have a freckle on the webbing between my thumb and index finger that I don't recall. I look up to even more wonders, the colors around me oddly brighter, the air in the back no longer stale and oppressive but interesting to me. I inhale the mix of old fryer oil, spilled beer and time and shiver a little.

The heat that spread through me from the meds has reached every corner of my body and I'm breathless.

When I pull myself together, pushing against the swinging door to return to my mystery customer, he's gone. Without a word, somehow without triggering the bell on his way out. In that instant, inexplicable as it is crushing, my heart breaks.

I have to catch the door frame to stop myself from wobbling, tears trickling down my cheeks, an ache inside me that washes over the heat like they belong together. It takes longer than it should for me to wipe my face, to sigh a shaky exhale and go behind the bar to retrieve his half-empty glass.

I have no idea who he was, but for a brief and shining time, he helped me wake up. That's exactly what it feels like, as strange as it sounds. My hands grip the edge of the bar and I lean in, breathing through my mouth, slowly opening and closing my eyes, waiting for the effects of the meds to wear off. For the world's brightness and color to fade again, to retreat and leave me in the sad, soft grayness that I realize has been my existence for all these years.

But it doesn't abandon me. If anything, it intensifies and as much as my heart is heavy in my chest, I'm lighter than I've ever been.

"Good drugs," I whisper into the quiet of the empty bar. And laugh.

When I reach for the half-empty glass of port, I notice a pair of hundred-dollar bills beneath it, way more than he owed. But it's the envelope resting against it that has me hesitating, fingers trembling again.

Anastasia. It's written across the front in bold, scrolling script.

I snatch it and tuck it away inside my t-shirt before I can think about it.

I have no idea what the letter contains. Or how he knew my name. Why he felt familiar to me. All I do know is that no one can see the letter. It's *mine.* Compulsion and protective greediness consume the moment, my hand pressing over the heavy stationery it's made of under my faded work shirt. I have no doubt whatsoever that if Mom or Jared or Dr. Matt were to discover this secret they would take it away from me and I will *not* allow that.

It's not until I'm turning off the neon light, my jacket zipped up, my winter boots on, that I acknowledge the irrationality of this entire night. I don't bother saying goodbye to Jared. I'm still angry and I don't know how I'll react if I do speak to him. Instead, I lock the front door, leaving the rest to him, and stand in the snow under the streetlight, far enough away from the bar that I feel like I'm alone.

And I *am* alone. The sidewalk is calf-deep in a wash of white, the streets empty of cars. I hear the rumble of a snowplow nearby, see the flashing amber lights as it passes one intersection down, but it fades and leaves me there in the quiet again.

I have to tell Dr. Matt about this reaction to the new cocktail she has me on. It's the responsible thing to do. I've had bad trips on her mixes before, so it's not the first time I've struggled with a fresh script. But this is the first time that I'm happy and despite knowing that it's a terrible idea, is it wrong I want to linger in this feeling a bit longer?

Even if it means I'm headed for a horrible crash?

The urge to run away has never been so powerful. So consuming that I sway in place and gasp a little laugh at the idea of just going, going, gone girl into the night and the cold and to *hell* with the consequences.

I don't, of course. That fantasy isn't rational. Logical. In line with my recovery from trauma. But it lingers regardless. I think it over as I walk home, trudging through the fluffy snow. It's slowed its fall somewhat, though flakes still quietly tumble in wonky clumps, the utter stillness of the night nostalgic and making the whole world feel like time itself has stood still. For me. For this feeling that I embrace physically as I hug myself and try not to laugh out loud.

The crazy girl doesn't get to laugh out loud where others can see her.

I almost regret it when the short walk is done and consider carrying on after all, rational or not. But Mom will be texting shortly for a check-in and I won't lie to her. I'll have to tell her, too, about this weird reaction. The shovel is still at the bottom of the stairs, which means she's gone to Clyde's instead of him coming to our place. I'm delighted. What is wrong with me? I'm actually humming to myself as I clear the walkway, the path to both of our downstairs neighbors' doors and then, finally, our stairs, exhaling misty breath when I'm done.

One last look up into the quiet snow and I finally go inside.

It's just as peaceful in the apartment. I carefully rack my boots, hang my coat, and head for my bedroom. Even here, the brightness lingers, the intensity of awareness, but I don't stop moving until I make it behind my door.

I can't latch it but I can close it and I do so, leaning against it. The scent of the new laundry detergent Mom bought hits me. I didn't realize how awful it is until now. But that doesn't matter. I'm hurrying toward my bed, sitting on the side facing the window, away from any possibility of prying eyes, fishing the odd envelope out of my shirt.

Anastasia.

I didn't imagine it. It's addressed to me in a scripted and elegant hand and I immediately imagine his ringed hand writing it with some elaborate fountain pen made of gold and polished wood. The question remains. How does he know my name? Curiosity clenches itself around my insides and my fingers shake as I turn the envelope over. There's a blob of hard wax on the flap, dark blue with silver veins in it, and I know the image in it when I tilt it into the light to get a better look.

The dragon on his ring, circling a diamond. Where

do I know it from? Because I do know it. I think? I shake my head at myself. It doesn't matter. I need to find out what's in the letter.

Now.

The front door opens. I hear it, feel the whoosh of air pressure changing, and instantly slide the letter between my mattress and boxspring. Wait, no. That's a terrible hiding place. My fingers fumble for my journal with its mess of articles that I've clipped about various treatments, sketches, starts to stories and other odds and ends that Dr. Matt suggested I look into as therapy. It's stuffed with enough unusual items that it might serve.

All the while I wonder, panic thudding a beat in my pulse, why it matters so much that no one finds out about the letter.

"Asta?" Mom is at my door, opening it and I'm turning to smile at her. I'm still shaking but I tuck my hands between my thighs to hide it, journal safely resting on my end table.

"Hey, Mom," I say.

She smiles back, a bit hesitant. "Are you okay, pumpkin?" She doesn't come any closer, watching with careful eyes. It's so intensely obvious to me then that she doesn't want the truth. I've suspected it through the dullness of the meds, but this is the first time I've actually seen it, experienced it. It's palpable between us and it hurts far more than I'll ever tell her.

"Of course, Mom," I say, standing and going to the end of the bed, closing the distance between us and blocking her view of my journal in the process. "I just got home from work." I forgot to text her in my focus on the letter. No wonder she's anxious.

"Thanks for shoveling," she says then, relaxing a little. "Mrs. Birch will be grateful in the morning." She won't. Our downstairs neighbor can't stand me, calls me the nutter in her heavy Irish accent, but whatever. "How was work?"

"Quiet," I say, now tense. Did Jared call Clyde? Say something about the stranger? My behavior? "We only had one customer after Clyde left, so when he was done, I came home."

She nods. "I wish you'd told me you were leaving," she said. "I would have walked you back." I exhale my relief slowly so she doesn't see it. That's all it was. "How are the new meds?"

I can't help the smile that crosses my face. "I think this might be a good combination, Mom."

Her return smile is hesitant. "We'll wait and see," she says. And hands me my pill case. The fake gemstones sparkle, reminding me of him and his ring. "Your sleep dose."

I go to her, pop the little lip without hesitation, and down the four pills inside without even water to choke them down. She seems surprised by my act but when she takes the case back, she hugs me. "Good night, pumpkin."

I squeeze her back. "Good night, Mom." I don't want her to see how eager I am. That's never good, either. But it's hard to hide it.

It's even harder to force myself to go to the bathroom, to brush my teeth as she watches me. To change into my pajamas as she observes, climb between the sheets. She leaves my door open and retreats to the living room. Which means, thanks to her full view of me, I also have to wait for Mom to go to bed.

I can't risk opening the letter until she does.

I'm suddenly heavy, my body tired, so I close my eyes, hugging my pillow to the sound of my mother giggling over a show with an accompanying laugh track. The soft conversation of the actors seems to stretch out and warp, the world tilting as I sigh deeply and feel reality fall out from beneath me.

The meds kick in and only for an instant does despair wake to weep over the truth. Whatever gift I was given tonight, whatever reprieve I was granted is gone.

Welcome back to the gray, Asta. Except it's not the dullness of nothing I'm used to.

It's fire. And it's come back for me.

CHAPTER SIX

—*I'm crying, sobbing, screaming for help, clutching something soft to my chest, the world around me hot smoke and flickering flames and as I cough the sooty death that tries to consume me, I see movement in the fire—*

—*a hand emerges, large and strong and reaching for me, grasping me firmly, pulling me out of the licking blaze—I know his face, love him, weep and writhe as he turns and tosses me out of the raging inferno—*

Someone is shaking me and I'm still sobbing, sitting upright, her hands squeezing my upper arms hard enough to make me cry out from pain. When I blink and inhale a sobbing breath I see her face in the dark, Mom's panic and fear naked for once, honest and raw. She shakes me so hard my head bobs and I have to pull away from her, gasping for air that comes in gulps and hiccups, the heaviness in my chest still present even if the smoke is not.

Though I can still taste it in the back of my throat. For some reason, when I have these nightmares, I can always taste the smoke.

"Asta." Mom gasps my name, hands reaching for me again but I push back, pressing my shoulder blades into the bare wall behind my bed, the pillow between me and the drywall scrunched into an uncomfortable mass. My mother's face is pale in the faint light from the hallway, her long hair a jumbled tangle from the sleep I've woken her out of, nightgown askew. I'm shaking so hard I can barely keep my teeth from chattering, squeezing my jaw tightly shut. Even then, my whole body rattles from the vibrations racing through me.

I'm coming down from the night terror, and it's not a happy ride.

"I'm okay," I lie when I can speak, pushing her hands away again when she tries to touch me once again. "I'm sorry." That's in a whisper because how many times can I apologize for something neither of us can control?

She's long ago stopped telling me it's all right. "We'll call Dr. Matt in the morning," she says in a cracking voice, standing and retreating from me, heading for my door. A door she again leaves wide open. "The new meds aren't a good fit."

I don't respond, staring down at my own hands in

my lap, hurting all over and still with that sickening taste of ashes making me want to throw up. I haven't had this nightmare in a while. Not since the last time I went into care. I know what Mom's thinking because I'm thinking it, too.

Please, let this not be like the last time.

Mom disappears into her own room, the 2:13AM time displayed on my beat-up alarm clock making me wince. Wait, didn't the meds work earlier...? I try to remember because something was different. Wasn't it? I shake my head at myself, slumping as I just focus on breathing. When I can finally drag myself to the bathroom, I brush my teeth to eliminate the majority of the smoke taste, though it never works entirely.

It's not the first time I can't bring myself to meet my own eyes.

When I lie down again, there's a burning sensation in the middle of my gut warning that I might need to go back to the bathroom, though the dullness of the medications I'm on seems to reassert itself, lulling me into nothingness. Flashes of the nightmare have me choking on tears, but I do my best to keep those to myself, my outbursts muffled in my pillow.

My father, my hero. A firefighter. He died saving me from a house fire when I was six years old and I've been broken ever since. I understand the trauma response thanks to Dr. Matt's explanations. I know my complex post-traumatic stress disorder, anxiety and depression all source from that one moment in time. That nightmare I relive sometimes, usually when the meds aren't working the way they're supposed to. Or when I'm close to the breaking point that means a stint in a hospital while they try to bring me back from the edge I can never quite escape.

I get it logically. But there's more I'm missing, I'm sure of it. Despite asking Dr. Matt and Mom, I've never found out what. If I could just remember, maybe I could break the hold the trauma has on me.

Despite the fight to think, to access memory, like always, I finally fall back to sleep. I wake to the sound of movement in my room, rolling over, bleary and soft, to find Mom standing over me.

"I have to go to work," she says. "In an hour. Can I leave you home alone today?"

Why wouldn't she? Did I do something to upset her? I slowly sit up on the side of the bed, accepting the pills Mom pours in my hand, taking them with the drink of water she forces on me. Something must have happened, I guess. Something always does. I rarely remember, though, which has to be frustrating for Mom.

The return memory of the nightmare has me stiffening. "I'm sorry," I whisper reflexively. "I'll do better."

She doesn't say anything. She hasn't bundled me up to take me to the facility, though. Or taken the day off work to run me to Dr. Matt. Mom's either decided I'm going to be okay after all or she's over it. Whatever her reasons, despite what she said in the early morning I'm only now dredging up from the depths of my drugged brain, she just leaves me to stare out the window into the whiteness of morning and the snowy backyard of our apartment building, trying to piece together the means to get out of bed.

My jeans are loose, but I can't find a belt. Right, she took my belts. Dr. Matt suggested it. I'm not a danger to myself, but they seem to think that's a smart thing, so okay then. I tuck my t-shirt into the waistband to try to hold my jeans up and shuffle out into the kitchen. Mom is frowning at her phone before she looks up and meets my eyes.

"I'll check in with you at lunch," she says, sounding irritated. "I can't stay home again, Asta." She tsks softly under her breath. I know that look. She's gone through almost as many jobs as I have, her new one as a receptionist for a local contractor thanks to Clyde. "Are you sure you're going to be okay today?"

I want to say, of course, I'm fine, but my lips feel thick, and my tongue is very pasty and heavy in my mouth so I just nod. The couch is close and I'm so tired. I might just lie down and close my eyes for a while.

Did I say that out loud? Maybe. She seems to accept the situation regardless. She leaves without hugging me or calling me pumpkin. I know she's unhappy, I just can't remember everything. Was it just the nightmare this time? Was there more that happened to make her so uneasy? Whatever the truth, it's on me like it always is. I wish I could remember. Saying sorry doesn't cut it when I can't even say what I'm actually sorry for.

It's not until Mom is at the door that it hits me.

—*a flash of flame, a hit of heat, the smell of smoke*—

And I'm inhaling sharply, memory returning, if only that. "I need to talk about the fire," I say. It comes out mumbled, muffled, but it comes out and Mom is turning toward me with a horrified expression. Is this what I upset her with? Did I ask about Dad before and forgot? I know better than to bring up the fire, Dad's death. She's never been comfortable with it. Honestly, neither have I. I almost retreat and mumble another apology but she smothers her reaction with a weak, sad nod.

"Go lie down, pumpkin," she says. "I'll be home later."

I watch her go, swaying in place, the memory fading as I fight to keep it. And then I'm suddenly back in my room, somehow on the floor of my closet. There's a box beside me, keepsakes scattered around me. I know these things, don't I? Photos, a few of them, his handsome and smiling face, me as a child in his arms. Articles and clippings from newspapers about his heroism, the small gold medal he won for saving a whole school bus of kids from a river single-handedly resting in a blue velvet box, lying in matching satin.

My father, the hero. *My* hero.

The bits and pieces I have left of him fall away, back in the box as I sag, aware one moment, in gray nothing the next. Wait, why am I surrounded by my bedclothes again? I have my pillow, the dark and quiet space of the tiny walk-in somehow comforting despite the horrible scent of something I hate. *Laundry detergent*, my mind whispers. It reminds me of roses and death. *His* death, the funeral home. The closed casket I was forced to stand next to. He was too burned, they said, for an open one.

Drift. In. Out. Gray, and then *blink*.

I curl into a ball so my feet are inside with me, all of me protected by the little bit of square footage and dimness and I wish I knew why I start to cry and can't seem to stop.

—as fire consumes me and his hand reaches out of the flames for mine, a hand I know, a hand I love—

—a hand wearing a ring with a dragon protecting a diamond in the middle—

CHAPTER SEVEN

I wake with a jerk, terrified and thrashing. It takes me a minute to untangle from my sheets and comforter, to realize where I am. By then, I'm on my hands and knees, surrounded by the clothing I've torn down from the hangers they dangled from, panting and sweating and shaking all over.

The bathroom is far away but I make it. Barely. The side of the toilet bowl is cold and soothing when I sit back and press my forehead to it, my insides burning, my throat raw from having nothing but acid to eject. I drag myself to my feet finally, brushing my teeth with barely enough vigor to do the job, staring at the blot of dark moisture on the front of my t-shirt so

I don't have to look into my own eyes.

Never look into your own eyes, Asta. I've made that mistake before. It's not something that ends well.

My timing is good, though. I muster the energy to rehang my clothing, to remake my bed. I've even stripped my shirt off and replaced it before Mom returns home. My effort might be minor but it's enough that she's smiling and falsely bright, brittle as always with me. Where did the day go? It doesn't matter. I'm just grateful I don't have a shift at the bar tonight. That was last night—

(wait, I worked last night, what happened, something happened—)

"How was your day, pumpkin?" She's cheerful enough that I do my best just to be still and not interfere with whatever has elevated her mood. She deserves that from me and I always do my best when I can not to upset her.

"Fine," I say, accepting my next round of meds, taking them automatically.

She inhales like she's going to say something, her smile twitching, failing. But when I force a little smile back, she beams at me that false sense of *everything's fine* that I try not to shatter.

If it wasn't for Mom taking care of me, I'd be utterly lost.

"Clyde and Jared invited us over for dinner," she says and now I know why she's in such a good mood. "Can you shower, please, before we go?"

A shower, sure. As the world wobbles, the gray an embrace I tumble into. I'm wet and then dry and the shirt I'm wearing now has that same rosy death scent I can't stand and it's cold but I don't mind, my feet shuffling over snow.

Wait, I'm in the kitchen at Clyde's and he's handing me a plate. How did I get here again? I smile at him, feeling dazed and take it but it slips from my fingers and there's a loud noise like something breaking—

Is Mom crying?

No, it's me crying and I'm in the dark, curled up on a sofa that doesn't feel familiar, that smells like feet and pizza, while I hear her voice somewhere, speaking. And Clyde's, too.

"I'm worried about her," he says.

"It's just Asta," Mom tells him with bright bitterness. "She'll be fine. Sorry about the plate—"

Reality wavers again, I'm cold, moving, stumbling. And then I'm blinking in our kitchen and Mom is leaning against the counter with a furious and frustrated expression on her face.

"—the first good man I've found," she's saying, and now she *is* crying and I'm crying again, too, but I don't know why because I don't feel anything, "don't screw this up for me."

I try to say I'm sorry but she's slamming her bedroom door, the hollow core thudding and bouncing back because it won't latch, and I'm swaying—

The scent of roses and death and chemicals are soft under my cheek as I close my eyes.

And let the darkness take me away.

I'm cold but I don't care. The heat inside me is devouring me, burning so hot I can't breathe. It's trying to consume me and it's going to finally, eat me alive and I want it to.

I want it to finally do what it's meant to.

But someone is screaming my name and I'm stumbling, falling to my knees, my hands finding no support as I fall face-first into cold wetness that does nothing to counter the fire, the burning—

Hands turn me over and I blink up into the night sky, Mom's face appearing over me, her terror mixed with fury.

"Asta!" She jerks me into a sitting position and only then do I realize I'm outside, in the snow, in the backyard, my mother shivering in her nightgown, the two of us in a snowbank while the fire still burns and burns inside me.

"Mom," I whisper. Reach out to touch her.

She flinches from me, jerking on me until I get up. Movement catches my eye and I see Mrs. Birch watching from her kitchen window, her small, pinched face a wizened apple of judgment and accusation but she doesn't matter.

Only Mom matters.

I follow her to the stairs, my bare feet leaving wet tracks in the snow, melting the cold beneath me. I should be frozen but I'm not, why am I not? Mom's winter boots thud on the steps as she tugs at me, forcing me to follow her up to our door. She pushes me through into the kitchen, panting and shaking from cold and emotion I can't seem to feel before she slams the entry closed and turns to face me.

"I can't do this anymore," she screams in my face. And collapses while I watch her fall to her knees, trying to muster something to comfort her, an apology, anything.

While the fire inside whispers its hunger.

CHAPTER EIGHT

Dr. Matt's office is cold like always, but I barely feel it. I'm still burning, and I don't want it to stop. What I do want to stop is Mom's meltdown as she leans aggressively forward from her own chair, not taking no for an answer when she barged in behind me and insisted the beautiful psychiatrist pay attention.

"She tried to kill herself!" Mom's gasping accusation has me shaking my head immediately, frowning and knowing my rebellious denial has to be showing on my face. Will likely only make things worse.

I can't help it. That's not at all what happened.

"Caroline," Dr. Matt says in her low, calm tone

that always makes me feel soothed and yet uneasy at the same time. Like she can tell a lie from a truth from a deception from an emotion without even trying. Mom stills and sits back, face pale but eyes bugging out a little. Hers are hazel, unlike my blue ones. I have Dad's eyes. Why did that thought intrude at a time like this? I have no idea but I cling to the memory of my father for a moment while the doctor smiles gently at my mother. "Asta doesn't seem suicidal to me." Her amber gaze turns to me, head tilting to one side. Why do I get the feeling she's listening to something? But to what? My heart thuds in my chest. It can't be that, can it?

I'm now thoroughly creeped out by my weird mental leap while she sighs softly.

"I didn't," I say.

"She had a nightmare," Mom says. "You know what that means."

The psychiatrist ignores her. "Tell me what happened," Dr. Matt says in her most reasonable voice.

I try to explain. Orderly thoughts I've been arranging and rearranging in my head since Mom dragged me back into the apartment and placed a frantic call to this very office had lulled me into a false sense of logical structure. Sure, I might have had a plan and a concise tale to tell, but the moment I open my mouth to share it?

It all falls apart.

By the time I'm stammering through mention of fire and the nightmares, of sleeping in my closet—to my mother's open horror—to finally waking in the snow, all of my previous confidence that I'll be able to convince Dr. Matt I'm okay winds down to one truth.

But I'm *not* okay, am I? That's the point.

I've only fed Mom's paranoia and I'm surprised she's not on her own litany of medications after everything I've put her through. But when my mother, staring at me like she barely knows me, mouth open and deep fear and hurt on her face, inhales to speak, Dr. Matt stops her with a single gesture.

"Asta," the lovely psychiatrist says with the same patience as always, "let's talk alone for a minute. Caroline?" She gestures at the door, waits for Mom to take the hint. Which she finally does, though she's staggering as she exits, purse clutched to the front of her puffy coat, the door thudding heavily shut behind her. Dr. Matt gives me a minute to decompress from that retreat before she sits back and nods at me. "It's going to be fine," she says. "Clearly, this combination of medications isn't working the way I hoped."

"Please, don't change them." I didn't mean to blurt that. I was only thinking it in my head and never intended to say it out loud. I collapse a little into my chair, huddling under her gaze. She's not angry or judging or anything that should make me feel uncomfortable and yet, I do.

More uncomfortable than I've felt with anyone. *Ever.*

"We can't just continue on, Asta," Dr. Matt says. "Not with a negative response to the combination."

I wish I could tell her about the warmth inside me.

The feeling of burning that is so delicious and has me stirred up, seeking out more of it. Not like any other time, like the spirals that led me to hospital stays and lost months. Instead, I just shake my head, knowing I have to look petulant to her.

"You're the one who says we should give certain combinations more time." I hold myself still and do my best to appear reasonable, logical. I think I actually succeed this time.

How do I know? She stops and considers what I said before speaking again. It's one of the things about her that keeps me coming back, even if she was always Mom's choice to begin with.

"Only if you're not putting yourself in danger," Dr. Matt says, holding up one elegant hand to stop me from arguing. Her nails in that awful shape remind me of my father's coffin, the closed lid of his casket, and I shiver. "Regardless of the reasons for that danger, Asta. Whether you intended it or not. The fact remains that you were out in the snow in your pajamas in the middle of winter." Her concern crosses her beautiful face. "Can you tell me why you ended up out there?"

I almost do. I'm this close to confessing that the drugs she's given me make me too warm, that I'm burning with the heat of a million coals now. The feeling reminds me of the fire, maybe, or has woken something in me that I'd thought lost. But I don't.

Not yet, a voice whispers to me. It's *my* voice, but it's not. It feels older, wiser. And now I'm afraid because one of my symptoms, one of the last pieces of the puzzle that falls into place just before I'm admitted to care, is hearing things.

Hearing *voices*. Why then do I trust that voice over Dr. Matt?

She waits long enough that I'm squirming before she pulls her prescription pad over to the center of her desk and writes something out in her neat hand. When she stands, she gestures for me to go ahead of her, ushering me out into the reception area. No next patient waits for her, at least, just the young woman she has as her receptionist. So Mom's insistence we just barge in the way we did hasn't interfered with someone else's care. Either that or the nice lady behind the desk—she's new even since two days ago, Dr. Matt never seems to be able to hang onto help— rescheduled so I could squeeze in.

That has me feeling very guilty because who am I to take someone else's precious therapy time? Not to mention Mom's continuing horror, lurking in the back of her eyes, in the jerking movements of her body as she stands abruptly like she's on springs and snatches the new script from Dr. Matt's hands before it's offered.

She doesn't even look down at it. "Will this fix her?" The demand for an answer has me cringing, wanting to crawl away into a hole and hide forever. I'm ruining everything and Mom's just doing her best. I owe her so much.

"Let's drop the anti-anxiety meds for now," Dr. Matt says. "And add in an extra SSRI with the ADHD combination." I've taken this one before. But I've lost track of all the different permutations. Still, it's hard not to feel helpless, like this is just another bandage over the gaping wound that is my broken brain.

Nothing will ever fix me. While the fire inside burns and burns.

Mom storms out, Dr. Matt gently squeezing my hand as I go. The drive is silent and tense, my mother's anxiety still elevated when she slams out of the car to get the new script filled.

I don't try to talk to her, staying quiet, huddling and being small so I won't set her off. By the time we arrive back at the apartment, Mom's overwhelm has retreated somewhat but she's still vibrating.

"I missed a day of work over this," she says in a tight, tense voice.

"I'm going to go to the bar today," I say. "I'll make up the difference." I won't. Mom's job at the construction office pays way better than some bartending job at a dive on the edge of town. But it's all I have to offer.

"Asta." Mom inhales through her nose, hands gripping the steering wheel though she turned off the car a full minute ago. "This can't go on, pumpkin."

"I know," I say. "I'm sorry, Mom."

She huffs like she has more to say but just shakes her head. "I'm going to take a night shift at the call center," she says. She picks up answering phones for help desks sometimes. She hates it, so we must need the money. "Text me every two hours." Mom exits the car without another word, taking the script with her. I follow more slowly, averting my eyes when Mrs. Birch peeks out at me through her curtains.

The fact that Mom doesn't argue with me about keeping my noon shift tells me she's really upset still. Otherwise, she'd insist I stay home and sleep. Instead, she dumps my pills, the pretty pink ones tossed into a baggie that she takes with her, before the new white ones join the blue, gray and green.

I take my altered dosage without argument, changing into a fresh staff shirt. Mom's already gone when I return to the kitchen. I stare for a moment at the sparkly pill case on the counter—

—*searing HATE bursts inside me and the fire that bubbled rages against it*—

I shudder and step back, gut in knots, panting through my open mouth until I'm able to regain control. Just as the first of the meds kicks in and the gray...

...washes...

...over me...

I'm surprised when I look up from the bar, rag in my hand, lucid and clear. What happened to the drug haze I've learned to function inside? I check the clock behind the bar and catch my breath. It's barely 2PM. I took my dose just before noon. There's no way it's run through me already.

Am I rejecting the drugs now? Has my body adapted to the complex cocktail to the point that they're no longer going to work at all? My hand aches where it squeezes the rag so tightly that my knuckles are white and I have to force my fingers to unwind. I should be terrified.

Why then am I elated?

I should go home, get another round of meds into me. But I don't. If anything, I feel great, that humming warmth inside me permeating everything. I'm smiling and chatting with customers, serving drinks, bussing tables and remembering everything. Including to text Mom before she can send me one first.

Clyde even comments at one point with a grin. "Someone's having a good day," he says.

I smile back and shrug. I can't help it.

There's only one other curiosity that seems to punctuate that weird and wonderful afternoon. Every time the door opens, I look up. It's not uncommon for me to do that, no. In fact, it's been a habit since I was a child. Dr. Matt says it's a reaction to losing Dad so young and that I'm just looking for him. I believed her then, when she explained it, and still kind of do now.

But it's not my father I'm looking for this time around. With each ringing reminder that the front door has been triggered I'm checking the entry, no matter where I am in the bar or what I'm doing, to see if it's him.

Him. Tall, dark and delicious. The *stranger*.

It never is and it's early evening by the time Clyde tells me to go home. I've dutifully texted Mom every two hours and even left her voicemail messages, knowing she'd check them but wouldn't have time to answer. I'm careful with my tone, keeping my voice as level and ordinary as I can. While the burbling happy that surfaced the day before struggles against me and wants to take over.

Maybe it's the medication after all, but I don't think so. That secret voice in my head, the one that sounds like me but older, more mature, assures me it's nothing like that. And yes, that means I'm crazy, crazier than ever, but I want to believe her when she laughs like she's been waiting for this moment my whole life.

To be *free*.

I'm about to go when a small group of young women enter. I know them enough to take them off Clyde's hands, one last order before I head out. I'm just approaching the table they've chosen when I hear the small brunette giggle.

"A whole *month* in Portugal," she gushes at her friends.

"You're *so* lucky," they all say in varying ways and degrees of jealousy.

She shrugs, dark eyes sparkling. "Can you imagine me? And a *backpack*?"

They all laugh while I hover, awkward and my insides now churning.

They're jealous of her, yes. I'm *dying* of *envy*.

I take their orders in a hurry, the girls barely acknowledging me past their drinks, huddling together to chatter about the pending trip. My feet stumble as I retreat, my hands shaking. Clyde notices, but I wave off his concern and hand him the slip I've written their requests on.

"You okay, Asta?" He really is the kindest man, one big hand squeezing mine. His skin is warm, usually far too warm when he makes gestures like that. I'm surprised that mine aren't the typical icy cold I'm used to but instead seem to match his normal temperature.

"Sure, Clyde," I say.

"Your mom said you needed to be home by six," he says. Then leans in and whispers like he's really trying to keep it a secret but is terrible at it. "You need to take your meds."

He has no idea but he might as well have punched me in the gut. I'm going to sob right then and there. The very thought of it has me backing away from him, though I hide my revulsion as I duck my head and grab my coat from the back. I'm jamming my feet into my boots when the thought crosses my mind.

Who says you have to take them?

Dr. Matt, of course. Mom. The facility that will strap me down and force me to if I try to avoid it. That's always their last resort, but seems to be my final stop no matter how hard I try.

Not this time, the voice says. *He asked you a question. You didn't answer it.* It doesn't mean Clyde. *She, not it,* she says. *And no, I didn't mean Clyde.* I fist my hands inside my coat pockets and barely nod to my boss on the way out because he can't know that I'm talking to myself in my own head. As nice as he is, he'll turn me in to Mom and I'll be back in a white room with a narrow bed and all the meds I can't handle and no hope before I can breathe.

What question? I whisper that fearfully into my own mind, knowing it means I'm nuts and I'm spiraling again but I don't care. I *don't.*

What are you doing in this stupid, sad small town,

Anastasia Fenimore? She sounds frustrated with me. *When you could be out there, living the life you're meant to live?*
I don't have an answer for her.
Because she's not real.
Right?

CHAPTER NINE

I don't intentionally *not* take my meds when I get home. It's not like I make a conscious decision to skip them or anything. I fully intend to, actually, except Mom's out and when I sit down to my computer, the whispering in my mind suggests I do something I haven't done in a long time.

I pull out the bottles in the cupboard and start researching the medications that Dr. Matt prescribed for me.

This isn't the first time I've done so, but I'd given up on it, frankly, with so many iterations of combinations making my head ache. It's been years, maybe? I blame the cocktail mix of anti anxiety, comorbid depression and ADHD methylphenidates plus SSRIs for my CPTSD for my lack of curiosity.

Except, as I punch each into the internet search bar and look at side effects, I'm frowning. None of them suggest any sort of numbness or mental fog, not even when combined. If anything, the new medications these days seem to have solved a lot of those issues. The final one has my stomach clenching, though, because I reject it immediately.

Schizophrenia. She has me on a pill to keep me from hearing voices.

Well, the woman in my head chuckles, *she's not wrong, is she?*

I sit back, shaking now and hugging myself. But this is the first time I've dealt with anything of that sort. Isn't it?

But is it? She sounds sad and now I'm afraid all over again. *Dr. Matt has made sure you'd never, ever remember. I wonder why that is.*

I push back from the table, closing the lid of my laptop, carrying it to my bedroom on shuffling feet. My hands are cold as I set it aside before lying down on the top of my comforter in the dark, arms spread wide, staring at the ugly popcorn ceiling. Light from the hallway makes weird little shadow mountains of the irregularities in the surface, prompting my imagination—

—flying, we're flying, there are clouds and wind and it's cold but I'm laughing—

My vision swims, tears welling and then trickling down into my hairline but I don't wipe them away.

Something is very wrong with me, broken inside me but I don't have the energy to fight it anymore.

Sleep, she whispers to me. *And dream.*

Is it wrong I'm terrified to close my eyes?

The nightmare starts almost immediately—

—fire, flame, smoke, choking me, the sound of screaming a wailing keen above the crackle, many voices lifted in terror around me—

—I can't see, can't breathe, stumbling into others who fall away, the heat is so strong I feel my skin sear, my hair curling up around my face as his hand reaches out of the licking death—

I'm choking as I sit upright, the last echo of my own screams dying in the room, the heavy banging from below me disorienting.

Until I realize Mom still isn't home but Mrs. Birch certainly is and the thudding I'm hearing is her broomstick against her ceiling, my bedroom floor, only falling still when I do.

No way I'll keep this from my mother. The nasty old lady downstairs will be calling her even now while I pant and wipe my face and nose on the crumpled tissues I fish out of the trash because the box by my bed is empty and panic won't let my knees work or my legs support me so I'm falling to the floor, dragging myself to my closet and pulling myself inside to hide in a corner, curled into a ball, chest on fire, shaking and shaking and shaking as I sob silently into a pillow so Mrs. Birch won't freak out again even though *I'm freaking out—*

Mom doesn't come. I have time to pull myself together, more than enough to still the shakes, to use the techniques I've learned to calm my thudding pulse, to breathe and tap on energy points and finally sag into surrender. When I drag myself out of the closet, I head immediately for the kitchen, my hands fumbling over the sparkling case of pills, palm full of small tablets that beckon me to oblivion.

You're stronger than this, the woman in my head sighs. *Oh, Asta.*

I take them all in a single go, emptying the part bottle of water that always seems to be on the counter to wash them down before making it to the bathroom. My hands are shaking again as I brush my teeth, wash my face, blow my nose. And welcome the wave of numb as it folds over me.

My choice, for once. Bed beckons and I don't argue. Or dream, this time.

A blessing.

She's standing over me in the morning light, face pinched and angry as I blink up at her, realizing she's been shaking me and that's the only reason I'm awake.

"Mom," I whisper, voice a crackling protest.

"You didn't take your meds," she snaps at me, the case in her hand. Like an accusation, sparkling in her clenched fingers.

"I did," I say.

"You missed a dose," she snaps, again thrusting the case at me. "I know, Asta. Mrs. Birch..." she trails off, looks away, her cheekbone and jaw tense in sharp relief in the bright morning sunlight reflecting from the snow outside my window. "I don't appreciate being lied to. Or woken up in the middle of the night at my boyfriend's house." Clearly, the worst part of the offense. Wait, she said she was taking a shift. She didn't? "Only to be told that you're freaking out. *Again.*"

So, the old lady did call. But Mom didn't come home. Or go to work like she said she was going to. She's not the crazy one, though. She doesn't have to tell me where she is or what she's doing. The fact that she felt the need to lie, though… a cold pit of fear settles in my stomach as I try to rise, to apologize yet again.

I don't get to finish.

"Maybe it's time we find you a new option," Mom says, backing away, face now flat and empty. "A new psychiatrist, since Dr. Matt has failed you so many times." I'm surprised to hear her say that. She's been All About Matt since I was a kid. "Or maybe it's time we take the next step." She pauses. "Asta." And exhales. "I don't think I can help you anymore." My chest squeezes tight because I know what's coming. I've feared it for so long, but can hardly blame Mom for it, can I? "Maybe it's time you go into care. For good."

Everything in me screams in denial.

Everything but the voice in my head.

Well, finally, she says.

CHAPTER TEN

No matter what the voice in my head thinks, this is a disaster and I need to make it up to Mom immediately, to convince her, to fix this. Because while the crazy inside me might not be afraid of going into care, *I* am.

I remember what it's like and I promised myself the last time it was the *last time*. Like I get a choice.

"Mom," I'm out of bed and wobbling in place, knowing I'm weeping but unable to stop the tears, to sound reasonable or logical which would probably serve me far better than this overwhelmed state. "Please. Please, don't." There's so much more I want to say, I need to say, but I can't wrangle the words that have turned to snarling, spitting vipers winding around themselves and fighting me off while my stomach churns and I struggle just to stay on my feet. "Please, I'll be good." That's a whimper. A little girl's whimper.

Whether I hate myself for being so pathetic or not, the plea seems to get through to Mom who freezes in place, horror crossing her eyes, mouth hanging open. When she moves again, it's to touch my cheek with trembling fingertips, though there's a hardness to her that I haven't seen before.

I'm at the end of the line with her and her patience. I have to figure this out or there will be no more chances. And it's clear I can barely make it with her. What hope do I have on my own?

The voice in my head sighs in disappointment while panic pushes her away. I'm on my meds. I will take more if I have to. Anything to make her go away.

So be it, she says. *But when the time comes, I'll be here.*

Does Mom know I'm hearing that voice? I don't think so. She doesn't show it even if the moment of conversation crosses my face. She steps back from me, extending a handful of pills she dumps from the sparkly case. I take them immediately, swallowing them dry, and for a long moment, we stare at one another across the few feet that might as well be a vast chasm divide.

Mom turns then without a word and leaves my room, door wide open. I hear her set down the case on the kitchen counter, the sound of shuffling, of fabric rustling, before the front door opens and closes firmly again.

She's gone. And I'm alone. Who am I kidding? I sink to the bed, face in my hands. I'm always alone.

I'm *here*, the voice says.

Go away, I hiss back. And urge the medications to hurry the hell up already.

The phone rings before the numb can take me over and I rise to answer it, heart heavy though I'm hoping it's Mom. "Asta," Dr. Matt says in her smooth, caring voice. "I just spoke to Caroline. Are you all right?"

"Yes," I say. "I took my meds." It's not her fault, but I'm feeling defensive, cornered, and I fight a sudden and furious sob. Only my free fist clenched against my mouth keeps me from letting it out, my body hitching with the need to release it. It's not fair. It's not *fair*.

"I'm going to have you double your dose of your haloperidol," she says. That's the schizophrenia medication, right? I recognize the name. I'm already reaching for the cupboard door and the bottle, opening it with shaking hands as I prop the phone between my cheek and shoulder. The cap is tight. The childproof seal might as well be a ten-digit combo lock I don't know the code to for all I'm able to open it. I have to stop and breathe and realize she's still talking. "It's going to be all right, Asta," she says.

"It's *not*," I tell her, knowing I sound panicked, unable to stop the horrible, painful sound of it coming through. The bottle rattles as I fight the lid, finally feeling it give way at last. Only to spill the small, peach pills all over the counter. "She's going to put me away."

"Asta." Dr. Matt sighs softly. "Come see me, please. Let's talk today."

I just saw her yesterday. Even she's going to give up on me at this rate.

I manage to sweep the meds into a pile and, wonder of wonders, back into the bottle, spotting one last one under the toaster. The cupboard door thuds on the rest as I put the bottle away, the little circle of pink with the cutout line in the middle waiting for me to lift it to my lips as ordered.

Don't, the voice whispers, pained and worried. *Please, Asta. For once, trust yourself.*

My fingers move deliberately, the tasteless tab on my tongue as I respond to Dr. Matt. "I'll see you shortly."

The voice in my head retreats. The whole world retreats. I vaguely recall going to my room, but then there are only fragments. Mom, wait, Mom came home? She's hugging me, crying. Telling me she's sorry, that she'd never abandon me while she helps me shower.

How did I get in the car? And then I'm cold but the fire inside me hasn't gone away so I'm sweating, why am I hot again? Dr. Matt's voice reaches me briefly—

"—sure we can sort this out," she's saying. "It's just another stage, Caroline."

"I don't know how much longer," Mom says. Stops.

"Let's have that conversation when—"

And then I'm drifting again and everything is soft, so soft.

This time, when the nightmare starts, I'm not afraid, for once.

—fire and flame and screams, so many people screaming, but why are they there? I am alone...? But no, I'm one of many, there are women all around me in thin, white dresses, their hair catching alight and they are terrified, collapsing, hugging one another, weeping tears that spark as their long, golden hair catches fire and they burst into flame—

—his hand reaches through the fire for me and I'm reaching back, my dad, but no—

—a ring, he's wearing a ring, I know it, the shape and form of it, familiar with a diamond and a—

—something roars, giant and red and shining, reflecting the fire, an amber eye lowering to stare at me, slitted center deathly black while the screams around me go on and on and the flames devour everything—

Remember, she whispers.

But the fire dies out and the softness returns and I'm drifting—

I'm tired. So, I sleep. I'm tired. It's dark and then light and then dark again.

Nothing's clear. Everything's soft and hazy. I'm so very tired. I just want to wake up.

Why can't I wake up...?

You have to choose to, she says, her voice so distant. *It's on you, Anastasia.*

On me. I can't rely on me for anything.

That's what they want you to think. There's a glow, gold and orange and white, growing in the distance. The sound is like rushing wind and crackles. *You can stay*, she says. *You can lose who you are forever. I won't stop you.* She's so sad, like *he* was sad. What does that even mean? *Or you can make the choice you said you'd make. You can choose to remember.*

Remember. It's just a word, but it rings in my mind like metal on metal and then the fire returns, slowly building and I'm grasping for it, taking it in both hands, feeling it burn me though it doesn't hurt. Not like I expected.

His hand reaches for me, the ring glinting in the flames and I take it. Firmly and with excitement and joy and all the feelings I'd forgotten all this time as I laugh out loud.

Because for a single instant in time that hits me like a blow, I *remember*—

Gloriously, gigantically, deliciously, I remember—

As the fire rages around me and swallows me whole.

CHAPTER ELEVEN

I open my eyes. I'm hot, burning up, but my feet are cold. There's a memory in the back of my mind, something about a ring and a hand but it's vanishing into the dark again, gone in a rush as I try to bring it back.

It doesn't matter. When I look down, I realize why my toes are tingling and wet. Brown grass covers my skin, my bare legs exposed to the night and damp chill. There's dew that's recently been frost, tips of the blades still white with the fading icy grasp of the cold. Wait, where's the snow…? The front yard is clear, the street, too, the faint light from the corner illuminating the cluster of flowers rising from the bed near the gate.

It's spring? One of my hands rises without my permission, wiping at my forehead, sweat slick on my skin before it drops again to thud at my side. How long have I been drifting?

Too long, the voice in my head says, sad and tired. *But you're awake again now, Asta. You have to stay awake.*

My whole body tingles, the memory of the fire raging still stinging though not painfully, more like a zinging pins-and-needles reminder of the return of circulation, on the cusp of hurt. It feels good, invigorating, the clarity of my mind's sudden freedom as shocking as the retreating heat.

I turn slowly and look back, at the stairs to the apartment. The front door is open, the kitchen on the other side dark. Mrs. Birch's curtain twitches, the old lady's pale face a moon of pinched concern behind the glass, but I don't worry about her right now.

Run, Asta, the voice in my head suddenly urges. *Just run. We'll figure it out.* She sounds desperate. *Don't let them—*

"Asta?" And then Mom is there, her hand on my elbow.

I can't help it. I smile at her, hug her. She's startled, but she hugs me back until I lean away.

"I'm okay, Mom," I say. "Sorry about the sleepwalking."

Good, the voice says, relenting. *Very good. If this is what we have to work with, so be it. Just keep her calm.*

I shouldn't be listening to her but I can't help it. I've tried their way and I've lost months. And the voice in my head makes way more sense now that I'm clear.

Clean. Tingling.

Mom hesitates, but I take her hand and lead her to the stairs, back up to the apartment. I go to bed again, nose wrinkling at the smell of my pillow. I need to wash it. Not just it, but my comforter, my sheets. My hair. Everything in my room stinks to me now, like I've been wallowing in something that I can't stand for another second.

My mother watches as I pull my bedclothes off and carry them to the washer/dryer combo in the bathroom. She doesn't say a word to me as I stuff them into the upright drum and start the machine. She even helps me as I retrieve fresh sheets and pillowcases from the closet, though I can't bring myself to use the old pillow. It's yellow and stained and disgusts me.

She doesn't protest when I put it in the trash. She even goes to her room and retrieves one of hers, handing it to me. "We'll get you a new one in the morning," she says. Her smile is sad, her eyes afraid. I know why. "The meds," she says, choking up a little. "The new combination."

I have no idea what she's talking about, though I can guess. I don't remember a thing about the last few months aside from bits and pieces. Dr. Matt must have found a combination that works.

This is all you, Asta, the voice says. *Don't give your power away.*

Mom seems to believe otherwise. Hope is a scarcity for us. We've both let it bond us together in the past. Mom's not falling for it this time. As for me,

I'm helpless to fight it. I should be afraid, though. Except the fear of the voice that speaks to me? I can't muster it. I'm not scared of her anymore. I *want* her with me.

This freedom, as long as it lasts? I'll savor it.

Everything is different now that the fire burned me up.

I sleep, maybe for the first time, in peace. When I wake, Mom has already started on my clothes, washing them all. We cycle through my whole wardrobe, even my winter coat and by the time the morning turns to noon, the whole apartment smells fresh and inviting.

And yet, Mom makes a call, whispers into the phone as I prepare lunch, and I hear her, know who she's talking to, when she says, "I know we've seen this before, but..." Pauses to wait for Dr. Matt to respond. "You think it's temporary?" Her voice falls. "Should I bring her in?" Another pause. "Thank you." When she hangs up, her brittleness is back.

But my optimism remains. "Dr. Matt wants to see me." I smile at my mother and will her to trust me for once.

As I'm trusting myself, for once.

She softens despite her worry. We have been down this road before and I've failed her so many times. If it's not the fire nightmares, it's worse. It's this. The up lasts long enough to break both of our hearts. I get a taste of what life should be like, just before I spiral into disaster and a stint in care. But it's different this time. I'm positive of it. Even if Mom is still afraid.

Everything is light and sparkling and I'm singing

along to the radio when we drive to Dr. Matt's office. I have my journal with me and, while Mom goes in to talk to my psychiatrist without me, I open it, pen in hand, and begin to write.

—about a girl among other girls, sacrificed to a dragon, only to be rescued by a man with silver eyes flecked in gold—

"Asta." I look up, surprised to find I'm six pages into an outline for a book that I barely remember, Mom's smile weak and worried.

"Coming," I say, closing the cover, tucking it away into my backpack and entering Dr. Matt's cold, dim office.

She's waiting for me, offers her hand and for the first time, hers isn't hot against mine. Weird, I've never noticed before. Is that why she keeps her office so chilly? Or is the warmth I feel what normal people feel?

Am I really coming out the other side of whatever it is that's swallowed me whole my entire life?

There's nothing wrong with you, the voice tells me.

Confirming that there is, in fact, still something wrong with me but that maybe fighting it off was the problem. Could it be I just need to go all in on the nuts?

She sighs but doesn't comment.

"Asta." Dr. Matt's kindness doesn't relent but I can tell she's worried, see it in the tightness around her eyes, in her soft smile's faint tension. "Your mother says the new combination is working."

"I feel great," I tell her, nodding. "Different this time." I glance at Mom who stands nearby, clutching her purse to her chest. Wait, that's real hope on my mother's face. Is she giving in to the chance that this might be over, too? "I think it's working."

Dr. Matt nods, but I know there's a caveat coming. "That's wonderful," she says. "We'll monitor your progress closely, all right?" I don't argue because I need to prove myself, I'm aware of that.

You have nothing to prove, the voice whispers.

"You've had bouts of respite before," Dr. Matt reminds me. "Not to burst any bubbles."

"I know," I tell her, a bright light in my chest humming. "But this feels different." It does. It *does*. "Thank you, Dr. Matt."

The voice huffs but I ignore it because she's going to make me laugh and then they *will* think I'm crazy. Know, I remind myself then. *Know* I'm crazy.

Because aren't I? I'll take it if I get to feel this way. "Let's take it slow," Dr. Matt says. "With hope."

Now, the voice says as my mother and psychiatrist smile at one another and me, *we can finally get to the truth.*

I should be terrified. But I've never tried this path before, never just given in, have I? When all other routes have been exhausted, all other shots taken, there's only one left to go.

Full-on crazy it is.

CHAPTER TWELVE

Spring has never been so beautiful before, though I barely look up from my laptop these days. When I do, I enjoy the gorgeous flowers blooming in the front beds, the heat of the sun on my pale, bare legs as I stretch them out between two lawn chairs in between shifts at the bar. I still have my job, as amazing as that is. I guess all of those years living under heavy medication means I'm able to function despite not remembering a whole lot about the past few months.

It's enough to make me pause and want to cry sometimes, but I don't allow it. If I am falling headfirst into full-out insanity, I'm going to enjoy every freaking minute I have access to before they throw me back into the looney bin. I know Mom's waiting for the other shoe to drop, dutifully doling out my medications to me every day, three times a day, meds I take happily, even with a kiss for her cheek and a hug when I do, while I carry on and live my life and feel like someone I only ever imagined I could be.

The sun is shining inside me as much as outside me and I'll take it for as long as I'm able.

The thing is, despite the mix of chemicals I'm fed, nothing seems to change my state of mind or presence. The burning inside me is far too powerful for that and almost seems to sizzle its way through whatever I take, melting it, turning it to ash and sending it on its way before anything can alter my mental state. I know that's not true, of course. It's the medication balance that's finally allowed me to be normal. I always wondered what normal felt like, without the mania that preceded my previous downfalls, that is. Now I know and I want more of it.

All of it.

The voice in my head is the only real stumbling block to my belief that I'm going to be all right. But even she's pretty quiet most of the time. It feels like she wants to talk, but I've chosen not to hear her most of the time. It's liberating to pick the points that she's allowed to interact, as annoyed as she seems to be by that power I've gained.

The only moments she shows up are when I'm starting to question myself (*I'm here, Asta*) and when I sit down to write.

The former doesn't happen often and it only takes

a few soft, firm words from her to return me to my happy optimism. Maybe I should encourage her to stay, to say more, but as soon as I'm equalized, I shove her away again. If that's what she's good for, if that part of my crazy can be used to increase my joy, I'll use her like any other tool at my disposal and be grateful for her.

Hey, I've been beat up and battered by my psychosis for a long time. I have no qualms turning the tables at last.

As for the latter, I credit my descent into creating, into writing what wells up and takes over, with my present state of blissful contentment. It's been barely two weeks since Dr. Matt's hesitant hope, my wakeful walk in the early May morning, the fire inside me winning at last. A week, and already I've finished the first draft of a twenty-eight-chapter novel I'm calling *Dragon Girl*. It's a dumb title but I love it. It makes me smile and sigh and hug my laptop when I think about it, giddy with delight.

Dad used to tell me stories when I was little and I adored it. I never thought I could do the same. I guess I just never had the chance to find out if I had it in me. Until now, that is. Like floodwaters bursting through an overfilled dam, words demand to be written and I'm not going to deny them.

The story is stupidly romantic and reminds me of the trashy novels with the bodice-ripping women and bare-chested men Mom always reads. Any judgment about that falls away, though, because whatever I used to think about romance is being redefined.

My book is filled with knights and damsels and fire-breathing creatures. Only the knights are the jerks and the damsel is the heroine and the dragon is the best thing that ever happened to her. Who knew?

Writing it feels like a memory brought back from the darkness, though I know it's just my overactive imagination finally given a voice and trust and time. And in that one single week of bursting creativity that devours every moment I have to spare, I dump out the contents of my soul onto the pages that unfold into chapter after chapter.

Leaving me wrung out but delighted like I've never known before.

Still, there's a very personal intimacy to it that made me hesitate the first time Mom asked to read it. I'm two days in, my rhythm established quickly, hands cramping from so much time on the small laptop keyboard.

Not to mention spicy scenes that make me blush when I read them over after not even remembering writing them.

"Just a few chapters, pumpkin," she said.

I sent them to her, held my breath as she printed them off, sat down on the sofa, read through the pages. Mom's continuing preference for romance novels means her approval could make or break me.

When she looked up that first evening with a breathless smile from the end of chapter three, I beamed back.

"More?" She laughed. I made Mom *laugh*. Of course, there's more.

I don't mind that she teases me when I get lost in my fantasy world over and over, that she sighs over the romantic relationship between the lead character and her dragon savior. That she giggles and whispers about the sex scenes that leave her fanning herself. If anything, the encouragement seems to bring us closer together.

It's almost painful to set my laptop down and go to work, but I do it anyway. I'm even different at the bar, Clyde joking with me, Jared keeping his distance. The patrons tip bigger than they ever have, I guess because I'm happy. Two weeks. I have a small bankroll of cash, stuffed carefully into a purple velvet bag I found behind the bar, in my top drawer. I should share it with Mom. But she gets my paycheck and I just want something for myself.

I put away for a rainy day or a trip, even. Because hope has a home again and I'm not letting it go.

It's hard to remember what I used to be like as I sit there in the sun and just breathe. Before sending off the last two chapters—now edited—to Mom before closing the lid of my laptop and going inside. I wave at Mrs. Birch. She waves back, her attitude vastly changed since *I've* changed, no more thumping on her ceiling. No more nightmares to trigger her protests, either. But the fire keeps burning and I'm done fighting it.

I'll never fight it again.

Mom's in her room, the sound of her printer chugging away reminding me that while this book is done, there's so many more to write. That a week of brain dumping my heart and soul out followed by a week of agonizing over the words there as I edited and edited and finally stepped away, has come to an abrupt finale that is just the beginning. That surprises me the most as I realize I've wrapped up the ending of this one. Have I found my thing? I'd asked myself that before with other creative projects, all suggested by Dr. Matt. Only to drop every single one either thanks to the drugs or despair or a spiral down to the dark.

There's no doubting this path, though. Not when my main character dies in her dragon's arms after almost eighty years together, only to reincarnate and return to him as she promised him she would.

Leaving the way wide open for me, for them. For the future I never thought I'd get to have. So many lives to write about. The perfect series setup.

I can't wait.

"Asta?" Mom pokes her head out of her room. She has the last two chapters I've just finished editing in her hands. "Get changed, pumpkin. I'll meet you in the car."

Right, I have a session with Dr. Matt. It's only my second one since everything started making sense and I can't wait to see her. I beam at Mom and dance to my room, tucking my laptop away before changing into clean jeans and a T-shirt. I even brush out my blonde hair, fix my ponytail, brush my teeth. Mascara, lip gloss. All while looking myself in the eyes in the mirror.

Blue eyes that smile at me like a normal woman should

Mom's out of breath when she climbs behind the wheel and doesn't look up at me when I greet her, but I don't bother asking what's up. For once, it's not me. We drive the whole way with me singing to the radio, Mom's silence finally making me uncomfortable as she parks and tries to get out.

I touch her hand, stopping her, wondering why she won't look at me. "Mom?"

"We're late," she says somewhat breathlessly, pausing one last second before getting out and closing the door. She's right and I'm being silly.

Careful, the voice in my head says, concern tightening my stomach. *Something's going on.*

She's overreacting. *I'm* overreacting. I shake my head at myself and follow Mom inside, seeing that Dr. Matt is waiting for me with a soft, sad smile.

"Asta," she says. "Come in, both of you, please. Let's talk about this."

Told you, the voice whispers.

I'm now tense and don't want to be. I don't like this feeling. Not after I've worked so hard to be happy. Two weeks of happy, surely I've earned more than that? But as I sink into the chair across from her desk, the familiar chill of her office eats away at my confidence and composure as Dr. Matt pulls something out of her desk and sets it on the surface.

A stack of paper. That Mom adds to with a shaking hand.

My book. It's my *book*. What's going on?

"Asta," Dr. Matt says, hands settling on top of the manuscript in front of her, weighty worry making

Mom's fluttering anxiety beside me feel like an attack, "when were you going to tell me you've been hearing voices again?"

CHAPTER THIRTEEN

It's clear that Mom's been sharing my book with Dr. Matt behind my back, but I never said a word about hearing the voice in my head. Where is my psychiatrist getting her information?

I need to go slowly, the woman inside me whispering caution again, but I'm angry suddenly, a wash of it heated with the fire that consumes the drugs I'm taking—in my imagination, at least—interfering with my normal quiet complacency.

"You had no right," I say to Mom before turning back to Dr. Matt. "That's *mine*." I jab a finger at the book. "You're the one who wanted me to find something to occupy me. I did."

Dr. Matt's fingertips tap on the surface of the stack of pages, those dark nails in their coffin shapes far too steady, too confident. "I'm worried about you, Asta," she says. "Your mother tells me you've done nothing but write this," she gestures gracefully over the pages with one hand before her fingers settle on them again, a mix of ownership and accusation in that movement that has my jaw clenching, "for the last two weeks."

"And work," I say. Defiance is a new thing for me, fresh and heated with the flames that I embrace. While the voice sighs and sits back, abandoning me to my fate. So be it. "Did she mention that?" I glare at Mom again before clenching my hands around the arms of the chair. This is not like me. I know I'm firing off and I need to stop but the anger has its own life and the waves of rebellion *can't* be stopped. Maybe I don't want them to. For the first time I'm happy, damn it, *happy*. Can't they just let me have that?

Even if I *am* hearing things?

"Your entire demeanor has shifted far too much, too quickly," Dr. Matt says, Mom nodding quickly in agreement, though my mother shrinks from me and I wonder if it's fear or guilt that makes her do so. She encouraged me. Let me think she was happy, too. Was it all a lie? A horrible betrayal? Deception where I only wanted love? "Asta, please. You know that we only have your best interests at heart." Dr. Matt leans forward, that kindness she always shows me unchanged, her voice soft and level. "If you are hearing voices again, I need to know."

"Because someone like *me*," I say with sullen

bitterness, sinking back in the chair, "couldn't *possibly* have written something like *that*," I point at the book she's so possessive of, "without help, right?"

She doesn't say anything. She doesn't have to. I know what she's thinking.

If you're done, the voice says. *We need to salvage this if we can.*

"Writing is an excellent outlet," Dr. Matt says then, looking down at the pages under her hands. Her control, really. My whole life is, I realize. My fate and the future sit there with the book she hovers across and there's nothing I can do about it. "But there is a line between passion and obsession, Asta. I fear this has become the latter and that you're feeding your psychosis instead of healing it." I don't respond. Is she right? I hate the doubt that surfaces, the hiss of the voice to stay with her. Because it's true, all of it is true.

I just stopped fighting it at last.

"It's just an escape," I say, making an effort. The only play I have.

"Is it?" Dr. Matt's gentle smile has sorrow in it. "Asta, do you believe this book is true? That you're the girl in it?"

She's read it. That offends me more than her possession of the paper version of it. And she's judging me for the words I wrote. I blink in surprise, make a face that I'm sure twists my lips in incredulity. Where did she arrive at that?

"And you call me crazy," I say.

It's meant to be funny, but no one is laughing.

Dr. Matt sighs, sitting back, finally releasing her

relentless hold over the pages. They sit between us, white sheets covered in tiny black letters, but they might as well be a wall of impenetrable brick and unbreakable mortar. "I don't like it when you lie to me, Asta. Caroline," she looks up at my mother while my stomach sinks and panic takes its place, "I'm afraid she's devolving again." Mom hitches a soft sob, but she's nodding while my head whips back and forth. This can't be happening. They have to believe me. "I think it's time we look at care. For the interim." Her amber eyes lock on me. "Until we can sort this new delusion out."

"I'm *fine!*" I shout that at the psychiatrist, half-standing. I'm not helping my case, am I? My near-hysteria needs to retreat. With a Herculean effort, I pull myself back from the brink. "I'm more fine than I've ever been. Mom." I appeal to my mother who won't meet my eyes.

"When were you going to tell us about this?" Dr. Matt pulls open her top drawer and retrieves the small, purple cloth bag. The one I found behind the bar. The one I've been using to stash my tips.

Mom's been going through my things. Why does that surprise me? I gape at the money I thought I could keep and don't know what to say.

Words tumble out without my permission. "I just wanted something for myself," I whisper. "To take a trip. We talked about it."

"Asta," Dr. Matt says with such chastisement I wince. "You know that's not going to happen. Especially now. Your delusions are not only driving you to psychosis, you're hiding things, hoarding money, hearing voices." She stands abruptly, handing over the bag with my tips to Mom who takes it with trembling fingers. I watch my mother tuck it away into her purse.

As fury seethes and replaces my panic. "That's *mine*," I snarl. I know how I sound but I can't help it. I'm over this, I'm done. I made it out the other side and they're not going to take my recovery from me. Why won't they listen?

The door opens behind me. I know what's coming but I can't suppress the fury that burns and burns. I shouldn't fight. I have to comply with the two big men in white uniforms under their coats. I've been on this ride before. Struggling just leads to more drugs and a lot longer in care.

But I can't let them take me without a fight. It's been so long since I had any fight in me at all, I just *can't*.

They're bigger and stronger and used to wrangling the psychotic. Still, I manage to dodge them both to the sound of Mom pleading and sobbing, Dr. Matt giving orders. I make it to the door.

Out of the chill of the room and the dimness and the suffocating judgment.

A needle bites into the skin of my neck as my foot passes the threshold, freedom never an option. It only takes a moment for the heavy medication to subdue my soul, to draw me down into the dark.

They can't do this. Please, don't do this.

I'm here, the voice whispers. *And I'm not leaving you*

alone.

For the first time since I accepted her presence, I wish she wasn't.

Then, nothing.

Nothing at all.

CHAPTER FOURTEEN

When the fire burns inside me and wakes me up, I reject it.

When she whispers to me from the gray place and tries to console me, I ignore her.

When my mother comes to visit, I refuse to speak.

How long? I don't know. I don't care. My life isn't my own and the hope I allowed myself, the moments of optimism and brilliance and joy are bitter now, shattered bits and pieces that cut me with their betrayal.

All that's left is the gray.

The meds must be working because the voice is gone now. So are the nightmares. And any curiosity, motivation, desire. I sleepwalk through the days and slumber without memory through the nights in the quiet of the place they've put me.

It's familiar because I've been here before, the white walls, the scuffed floor tiles of industrial vinyl, the curtainless window in the small room with the metal bars outside. The cafeteria when they let me visit, the common area I hate because I'm not alone. No, I don't want to play checkers or listen to the mumbled madness from my neighbors or participate in group or take my meds. I just want to go to the darkness and never come out again.

Just leave me alone.

He shuffles toward me where I sit by one of the big windows overlooking the garden. It takes a moment to realize it's Jared but when I do, I feel my face frown at his arrival.

"Hey, Asta," he says. Swallows hard. I can't stop staring at his Adam's apple as it bobs up and down. It's horrifying and fascinating at the same time. "I'm sorry," he blurts then, hands clasped in his lap, fingers fidgeting. "I shouldn't have told Dad about your tips." He twitches, sitting back and then forward again. "I didn't know they'd do this to you."

If I could muster anger, I would, maybe. Then again, maybe not. What does he want? I have no way to absolve his guilt.

He reaches into his bag and pulls out something I should recognize. Again, it takes a bit, but I finally do as he lays my journal on my lap. Now I'm locked on the hearts and flowers and stars I drew on the cover once upon a time, stickers outlined in marker, another of Dr. Matt's craft projects that served a purpose. Wait, how did he get it?

I don't remember speaking out loud, but I must have because Jared shrugs, a jerking motion that precedes him standing abruptly. "You left it at the bar," he says. "I thought you'd want it. Sorry, again." He spins and exits in a rush, almost colliding with an orderly who reacts badly, his tray of medications tipping, rescued from falling at the last moment.

But I've already forgotten Jared. My hands slide slowly over the cover of the journal, the texture of the stickers rough under my fingers, one of the stars peeling from the top right corner. Something wet splashes on the heart in the middle and I reach up to touch my face. My fingers come away wet.

I think I'm crying.

Oh, well.

A hand snatches at the journal, narrow wrist clasped in a plastic id bracelet like mine. The girl on the other end of it tries to take it from me. Tries to steal it right from my lap.

Why does it feel like I'm so far away? From the screaming, the clutching of the book against my chest while I watch, detached, as the body I inhabit lashes out, punching the thief in the face, pushing her to the ground, shrieking bloody murder that only ends when two orderlies pull my physical form away.

The jab of the needle is a distant thing. My heart aches for one brief, painful pulse.

And then the darkness again. I'm not alone,

though. One of the orderlies sits next to me. He holds something in his hands. It's long and thin and pale cream and I recognize it, don't I? *Yes*, with a hissing hit of heat that startles me and forces me upright.

He spins on me, eyes wide, bulky body leaning toward me, holding out the envelope. The one with the wax stamp on the back, blue with veins of gold, a dragon circling protectively around the diamond in the middle.

The one I'd forgotten until now.

Until right this second as fire rages through me.

"You want this, huh?" He grins at me, looking down at my chest. "I'll let you have it. If you'll give me something. Be nice, Asta. Be real nice and I'll make things nice for you, too."

How is it he's on the floor? Why is his nose bleeding? He's scrambling back from me as flames consume me, eat me alive, terror on his face.

"I'll tell everyone," a voice says from between my lips, but it's not my voice. "They'll believe me, too. Get out. Now."

He scrambles to escape while that voice sits my body down, sighing deeply. She turns the letter over in my hands, shaking my head for me.

"All right, Asta," she says. "That's enough of that. Time to wake up, now."

I'm on fire—

When I open my eyes, it's dark outside, dark in my room, faint light coming in from the small window in the door. It takes a moment to realize the gray is gone, the weight of the medications. The shift in perspective has me clenching, waiting for the inevitable that doesn't come.

I groan as I roll over and sit up. My body is sore, weak. How long have I been lost here this time? I make it to the small bathroom and wash my face, brush my teeth, even manage a quick look in the mirror. I'm gaunt, skin faintly gray. The ugly white scrub top I wear isn't doing me any favors, nor is the mass of blonde waves that have matted around the elastic someone used to tie my hair back.

It takes a long time to brush it out. To resecure it with a new elastic. I'm wobbly with fatigue by the time I shuffle back to bed and sit. There's little on my nightstand but a bottle of water, a small picture of my mother in a plastic frame—no glass.

And the journal. *My* journal. Not a dream or a delusion.

I clutch it to my chest with a heaving sob that hurts but makes me feel alive. And only then do I remember. The letter. How did I forget the letter?

They made sure of it, she says. *Find it, Asta. It's important.*

It takes me a bit. It's not in the journal, though I flip through all of the pages. Nor is it in my bed, tucked amid the messy sheets, the thin blanket. I finally drop to my hands and knees and look under the cot, spotting the pale rectangle of paper where it's slid out of sight.

I'm so wrung out that it takes a fair amount of grunting and wriggling to reach it, the coolness of the stationary soft under my fingertips. I'm panting by the time I sit down on my bed again, the envelope in my lap.

Don't let them find it, she says to me. *They'll take it away and we'll lose our chance.*

Our chance for what? *I won't,* I respond, examining the crest pressed into the wax with touch and sight. I lift the envelope to my nose, the faint scent of him, of deep woodlands and dark chocolate and the smoke of a thousand fires. I remember him now. The handsome man with the silver eyes flecked in gold. Thinking of him has my heart beating faster, the fire burning hotter. I remember what it feels like when his hand strokes my hair away, cups my face.

I never knew his name, but his touch felt like something I could never forget. His fingertips on my cheek, his sad, beautiful smile. The faded scent of him makes my heart ache.

He's waiting. She sounds almost panicked, frantic. *I just hope he hasn't given up on us.* She hisses something inside my mind that has me twitching. *I'll never forgive her for this.*

Waiting for what? I almost don't want to break the seal. It's so beautiful. But she's in control and it makes a soft cracking sound when she snaps it in half, perfectly right down the middle, separating the flap from the rest of the envelope.

Just read it, she says. *And then we'll talk.*

But I hear a footfall at the door and tuck it away just in time, between the pages of my journal. I turn as the light floods in and two orderlies appear. Not him, though. Not the one who I now know tried the unthinkable.

He'll not return, she says. *I made sure of that.*

Her assurance has me smiling.

The orderlies exchange a look and seem to relax, one holding out my medications. I take them as she speaks quickly in my head.

Asta, listen carefully, she says. *They're going to try to silence you again. I'm not going to let that happen.* Her grim assurance has me nodding. I hope they think I'm addressing them and not her. Funny how I trust the delusion more than the people standing right in front of me. More proof I'm a lost cause. *I'll free you again, I promise. Do as you're told for now. We'll make this work.* She's desperate again as I upend the little paper cup's contents into my mouth and sip the water they provide me. *I swear it, Asta. We'll see him again.*

I can't stop smiling, even as the gray takes me.

To the scent of the forest and chocolate and smoke.

CHAPTER FIFTEEN

I wake to fire, but not the kind I expect. There's a TV in front of me where I huddle in an easy chair in the common room, a festive hearth crackling on the screen, one of those Christmas channels with its perpetual flame burning.

Wait. It's Christmas?

Asta. She's there with me, her relief sharp and bright. *You're awake.*

Hello, I sigh to her. *It's been a long time, I take it.*

You have to stay with me, she says. *I can't keep burning you up.*

The orderlies are making their rounds with their little cups of pills and water. *Can't you just...?* I wave one hand over my lap. I'm so tired, my body weaker than I remember, even more than the last time I was awake. How long has it been? I have no way of knowing.

I need you to pretend, she says. *Can you do that?*

I can try.

It's easier than it should be to fake it. I'm not a problem to them anymore, I suppose, or they're being lax in their observations. It helps that one of the other residents throws a fit as I'm accepting my cup. I quickly dump the contents into my lap and cover them with one hand, sipping water and showing my empty mouth before they move on. The little collection of pills goes into my robe pocket and that's that.

I should feel a thrill of excitement at the successful deception but all I feel is tired.

My feet shuffle in my slippers as I'm sent back to my room, the common area closed for the night, all of us crazies tucked neatly to bed. I fight panic when I realize my journal isn't there on my nightstand where I left it, but she quickly reassures me.

The bathroom, she says. *Hurry, Asta.*

I cross to the small space, looking around.

The tile in the back under the toilet, she says.

I'm on my knees again, the cold floor hard on my bones, but she's right. The tile is loose and when I pry it up, a fingernail tearing in the process, the small gap there reveals my journal. Safe and sound. Wow, I've gone above and beyond nuts this time. Doing secret things without my own consent or assistance.

Oh, stop that, she says. *There's no time to waste.* I feel her urgency. But it's impossible not to take a moment and hug it to my chest, to rock with it and let the tears of relief fall. *I know*, she says with bottomless sorrow. *I'm so sorry, Asta. You have to get up.*

The bed is an impossibly long way away, but I make it and flip open the journal without waiting for her to instruct me. I find the envelope, still safe. *Thank you*, I tell her. She took over, hid it. There's no other explanation.

And I'm fully crazy now.

You're not crazy, she snaps. *Asta, for goodness sake, read the letter.*

At long last, with shaking hands, I slip the page out of the envelope and open it, tilting the single sheet sideways into the light as I unfold it and begin to read.

While she whispers the words out loud in my head. But she quickly turns into him and I'm falling into the cadence and tone that is his deep voice:

Anastasia,

I fear you were right. Your worry came to pass. I've left this far longer than you ever did, though only to ensure that it was necessary. I should have let you be. It's selfish of me to lure you back to this when you're finally free. But a promise was made. I will always fulfill my promises to you, no matter the cost.

If our time is done, so be it. I wish you well. Know that you have changed everything for me and that of all the things I am grateful for in this endless existence of mine, your presence in it is the most precious.

Should you remember sometime in the future what we've been to one another, find me here:

helios@eliasveles.com

Love, El

As his voice fades, she sighs deeply, my whole body heaving with it.

There's still time, she says. She's almost in tears she's so relieved.

Who is he? I choke on the question. I should know. I need to remember. But there's nothing *to* remember. My delusions have never been so tangible before. So Mom and Dr. Matt were right to lock me up and douse me in chemicals and throw away the key.

Weren't they?

She's quiet for a very long time before the strangest sensation passes over me and then through me. It's like she's hugging me, even though that's not possible. She's not real, none of this is, I'm just nuts. When I look down, my own arms have risen and are embracing me, logical explanation achieved.

Except there's nothing logical about any of this.

Asta, she says, *we need to send an email.*

To him, obviously. *You know it's not real, right?*

Stop that, she chides me. *Have a little faith.*

She has to know that's a giant request. *Who are you?* I almost don't ask. I don't want to know. But I do want to, at the same time. I'm terrified of what she'll say.

My fear is confirmed when she responds. *I'm you, of course*, she says. *Or the you that used to be. His version of you. And, with the grace of all that is powerful, I will help you reach him again.*

It's true, then. I've passed the point of no return from my insanity.

She tsks softly. *Then you might as well go all in, right?*

I laugh, weak and helpless. "I guess," I whisper into the dark of my room.

We need to send that email, she says. *Asta.*

Okay, I say. *How? There's no way they'll give me access to a computer.*

We'll figure that out, she says.

What would I even send to it? I sag backward, the letter on my chest, staring at the ceiling. Why am I hopeful all over again? There's nothing to be optimistic about.

I remember, she says. *Love, Anastasia.*

It takes a second for me to realize she's not talking to me but answering my question. *That's it?*

That will be enough, she says with so much confidence I feel it in my bones. *Trust me.*

I do. Heaven help me. I *do.*

Tomorrow, I say. *I'll find a way tomorrow.* This has to end. Either he's real, this voice in my head is telling me the truth and there's some freaking conspiracy going on that I don't know about, or…

I really am cracked fully down the middle, never to be repaired.

One way or another, I need to know.

CHAPTER SIXTEEN

I manage to make it all the way to breakfast without anyone knowing I'm not medicated. The orderlies aren't paying attention at all and I palm yet another set of pills that go into my robe pocket with the ones from last night. It's a small victory but I'll take it because I have to have my wits about me today.

If I'm going to send an email to an imaginary man who the voice in my head seems to think wants to hear from me.

That has me sniggering to myself while she sighs but lets me have my delusions. The food is bland but it's plentiful, so I make sure I fill up on toast and orange juice. I'll need the energy, the scrambled eggs tasteless in my mouth. I eat with grim determination that I have to tamp down when I see one of the nurses watching.

Right. I'm supposed to be listless and out of it. Way to blow the whole thing before it even begins, Asta.

She wanders off when I sit back and stare at the floor for a solid minute and now I'm horrified about how much time I've lost.

Don't fret over that right now, she says.

What do I call you? I finish my orange juice with as little enthusiasm as I can muster. Who knew I had acting skills?

Zia, she says. *If you feel the need to call me something. Now, let's find a computer.*

There are such things available, of course, but without internet access. I putter over to one of the ancient desktops in the common room and sit down at it, frowning at the slim selection of options. *I don't think coloring or connecting shapes is going to cut it*, I say.

Agreed, Zia says. *Are you sure you can't get online?*

I'm far from a hacker, but I can check, I guess. The settings screen chugs while I do my best to keep my eyes on the watchful orderlies without them noticing. And almost meep in excitement when I realize the truth.

The wireless connection is still available, I say, almost hopping up and down in my seat.

Deep breath, she chides me, but even she sounds excited. *Can you get an email out?*

I know I have an account, but there's no way I can

access it. I don't even remember the password. *I'll have to make a new account*, I say.

That will take too long, she says.

Good thing someone already has. I grin at the screen. Someone's been using this computer to contact the outside world. There's an account already logged in. One of the orderlies? A patient? I don't care. It doesn't matter. All I know is, their mail account is ready and waiting.

Quickly, Asta.

I open a new email and type in the address, *helios@eliosveles.com*. My memory is kind of cooked, but I remember that. I'm half expecting someone to swoop in and stop me as I rapidly add the message to the body. *I remember. Love, Anastasia.*

Send it, she says.

I do, clicking the mail button. And sit back with a rush of excitement and accomplishment that has us both warm and giggling.

Now what? I shut the computer down, careful to log out of the internet again. Surely, I didn't just get away with something here? It has to be a delusion.

Now, she says, not bothering to correct me, *we wait for El to come get us.*

If you say so.

The day drags by without the drugs to lull me. She doesn't even have to suggest that I fake taking my afternoon dose. When they return me to my room, I flush everything down the toilet and take a seat on my bed, hugging my knees to my chest.

I hope he comes soon, I say. *I don't know how long I can pretend.*

She's quiet for so long I wonder if she's gone. *Asta,* she says. *Your journal.*

I look down at the end table. The empty end table. As my door opens. And Dr. Matt steps through. With my journal in her hands.

Too easy, you idiot, she growls. Is she talking to me? No, I get the impression that's a more personal attack. Then, *Don't say anything,* Zia whispers to me. *Not a word, Asta.*

My stomach clenches as I watch my psychiatrist cross the room toward me, holding out my property. She's smiling that sad smile of hers, but her amber eyes are tight around the edges, and she's clearly upset.

Even more so when she slips the envelope out from between the pages.

"Asta," she says in that disappointed tone of hers, "we really need to talk."

Not. A. Word.

I follow Dr. Matt out of my room and down the hall, into an office. It's not her office, not chilly like I remember, spare on the decorations and personalization. But she dominates it like she always does and now I'm sweating, fire inside me bubbling and burning as the voice in my head seems to perk and listen as closely as I do.

"I had hoped," Dr. Matt says, "that you might have given up on this delusion. I can see now that isn't the case."

"That's mine." I blurt that before I can stop myself and ignore Zia's grumble of protest.

"It's only feeding your psychosis," the psychiatrist says. "Asta, really." She exhales heavily, frowning, finally showing some irritation. "I've been so patient. Your mother has been beside herself. We've tried everything. But I think it's time to accept that only tough love will shake you out of this situation. It's all we have left."

Stay with me, Zia whispers. *Whatever she tells you, Asta, it's a lie.*

I try very hard to believe her as Dr. Matt rises and goes to the door. I'm shocked when I see Mom there, holding a small cardboard box. She won't look at me as she hands it to Dr. Matt, entering quietly and standing in the corner as the psychiatrist brings her burden to the desk and sets it in front of me.

When she flips the top open, she speaks. "You think someone sent you this letter," she says. "Is that right? Some mysterious man?"

"He's real," I say. "Ask Jared." He saw him. That much I know is true.

"Yes," Dr. Matt nods as she starts to pull items out of the box. Items that make me flinch as I take them in. A sleeve of paper. A fancy box of envelopes made of familiar cream stationery. A wood-handled stamp. Blue wax. "The man was real. The perfect stranger around whom to build your delusion. As is always your way, Asta." She presents the items in a line on the desk before sitting next to them, crossing her arms over her chest. "Your mother found these in your room," she says.

Asta, Zia says. *She's manipulating you.*

Dr. Matt pulls out a printed sheet from inside the box, showing it to me. It's from an online store, all of the items listed on it. In my name. Paid for on Mom's credit card. "You fabricated this entire thing," she says so gently that I want to weep as I take the page from her with trembling fingers. "You built this entire delusion, Asta. A fantasy to hide in. The book, the letter." She pauses, sighs. "The email."

My head jerks up as Zia hisses in my head. *She's lying*, she says.

"Yes," Dr. Matt says. "I know about the email. I gave you access to the opportunity to send it, Asta. I wanted to see how far your delusion had taken you." She's shaking her head in regret. "You proved to me that nothing we've done up to this point has helped you."

No, Zia whispers. *Don't listen—*

"Asta." Mom kneels next to me, hands clutching my wrist, tears running down her face. "Pumpkin, please, come back to me." She sobs once, her forehead pressing against my arm. "Please, baby."

It's like a hand has reached inside me and torn out my soul. "I made it all up," I say. I should be more surprised. Instead, I'm gutted.

And Zia... is gone.

Because she was never there to begin with.

"No one is coming to rescue you," Dr. Matt says. "It's up to you to get better, Asta."

She has no idea how firmly she's crushing me under the weight of the truth. Mom, however, delivers the final blow. When she slips her hand into her purse and, with a nod from Dr. Matt, hesitantly deposits a photo into my lap.

I stare at it, a camping trip in the forest. A little blonde girl hugging her father—me, my father—with one arm around his neck. While the other clutches—

"You've always been fascinated by dragons," Mom chokes. "That's the one your father gave you. Your favorite." The blue plush toy is almost as big as I am, with a giant grin and silver eyes, shining wings and a coiled tail. "Elliot."

Elliot.

El.

Oh. My. God.

I crush the picture to my cheek, tears smearing the shining surface. *El.* I remember that stuffy. How did I forget it? Dad gave him to me for my birthday. Two weeks before—

—the fire and smoke—

—along with a box of treats. In the woods—

The scent of the forest and chocolate and smoke.

"Dad," I whisper.

"This isn't the first time we've been here, Asta," Dr. Matt says.

"What?" I look up, choking on my grief, on understanding. It's all been a lie after all. The psychiatrist stares me down, her amber eyes seeming to burn. But there's no fire there, just my old sorrow and my brokenness seeing things that don't exist.

That's all this is, in the end.

"Do we have to?" Mom's crying, too, looking up at Dr. Matt.

"It's time, Caroline," the psychiatrist says. "One more time."

Mom stands up, squeezing my hand. "I can't watch. Not again." She spins and leaves the room, the door closing behind her.

Dread fills me up to the brim and I can't breathe, I can't move, frozen in place and in time as Dr. Matt leans close to me, face inches from mine.

"You need to remember, Asta," she says. "What really happened that night." She pauses while panic turns to hysteria that spins into terror. "What happened to your father."

I can't speak, just shake my head. I'm so afraid, but what am I afraid of?

"Every time we face it together," Dr. Matt says, "you break. But there's no other way. We have to keep trying. Are you ready to try again, Asta?"

I have to know. Heaven help me, just like before.

I nod.

You're not alone, Zia whispers. She hasn't left me, then. I'm not sure that's a good thing.

As Dr. Matt begins to speak.

CHAPTER SEVENTEEN

"I had hoped," the psychiatrist says, still seated on the edge of the desk, knees almost touching mine, far too intimate for my liking right now but without the ability to ask her to back off, "that we might have had a breakthrough this time." She crosses her arms over her chest, her fitted suit straining against the action. I stare at the creases created over her biceps as she goes on, lost in the valleys and shadows of the dark fabric's distress. "For the first time, you supplanted your usual fixation on your father with a stranger's identity. Which, I thought, meant you were finally distancing yourself from the trauma. Your mother worried it was just another layer of your delusion, but I had faith in you, Asta." She sighs deeply, the gold of her necklace glinting in the terrible, harsh light of the florescent bulbs overhead. Her beauty feels fake to me in their glow, like she's a construct pretending to be a human being. But it's just the nasty lighting.

Is it, though? Zia's whispered question lingers while Dr. Matt carries on.

"The fire, your father rescuing you," she says, clearly knowing each word lands like a blow that I flinch from, delivered in that odd accent that triggers something I just can't recall, "memories that you've woven into a narrative that sent you spiraling, looking for him to save you from your own mind." I'm used to her psychobabble, yes. But something has me paying attention this time. "The fact you've replaced your father with this stranger you've now built an entire book around..." she drops her hands to her sides, gripping the desk on either side of her skirted hips. Why are her knuckles white? "This new fantasy could have been the means to bring you out of your delusion, if only you had accepted that it was just that. A fantasy."

I look up and meet her eyes again at last. The fire I imagined in them still burns. Which means my crazy hasn't abated. But I'm not mad about it. If anything, I'm furious for other reasons. "You manipulated me into this," I say. "You could have just told me the truth."

Her full lips purse, that disappointment returning. It doesn't land the way it usually does, though. What right does she have to judge me? Yes, it's probably the make-believe Zia in my head muttering those words, making me rebel. But I don't care.

I'm so over all of this. Fine, I'm crazy. Just let me be, lady.

"Asta," she says. "I need you to tell me what you remember about that night."

This is the lynchpin, Zia says, loud and clear. *Pay attention.*

I shake my head, more at the voice than at Dr. Matt, but I answer regardless. "I don't remember much," I say. "Probably because of all the drugs you've been giving me." Sullen, bitter, childish.

Unworthy of you, Zia sighs.

She can go to hell, too, for all I care.

"Asta," Dr. Matt says in that same tone, unfazed by my attitude. "What do you remember?"

I sit back, the picture of Dad and me in my hands, the stuffed dragon I barely recall stirring something inside me that aches like nothing ever has. "Fire," I say, my voice cracking despite my newfound resistance. "And Dad reaching out to me." The hand with the ring, though, not Dad's hand. That's the new part. And screaming, *voices screaming, women in white dresses, their hair aflame. An amber eye, bigger than I am, unblinking with its slit of a black pupil contracting—*

She shifts positions a little, bringing me back. "Before that," she says. Why does she suddenly sound as intense as I feel? And her accent, it's thicker, deeper, almost harder to understand her. I twitch, the photo in my fingers bending a little under the pressure. I look down at the dragon stuffy in my little arms and frown at it.

"Dad gave me Elliot," I say. "For my birthday." Along with a box of my favorite chocolates during one of our weekend camping trips. I loved the gift, hugged the plush dragon tight. It's a flicker, but that's enough. "I named him El." I named him El. It was Dad who misheard and called him Elliot.

"Good, Asta," Dr. Matt says, breathless as she encourages me. She's regained her control of English, swallowing her own language's influence again. "Go on. What else."

"We... were supposed to go camping." Another flicker, of a pile of gear at the door, Dad getting a call. "We stayed home." I don't think I ever knew why. "I woke up to smoke." *And fire, and Dad's hand in the flames—*

Dr. Matt's fingernails slide over my wrist, the scraping feeling of them making me shiver. I've never noticed her scent before. Or maybe it's memory because she smells like smoke, too. And dust, mixed with something metallic I can't identify. Under the perfume tones she wears, she smells like my past.

As fire burns and burns in the back of her amber eyes—

"Asta," she says. "How did the fire start?"

I shake my head, brought out of the brief flickers of memory. "I don't know," I say. Why is my stomach clenched all over again?

She squeezes my wrist in her grip, stronger than I expect, her nail tips biting into my skin. "You *do* know," she says. I stare at her glossy, dark lips as they form words, barely able to hear her past the crackle of

118

fire in my ears.

And Zia's voice speaking over her.

Pay attention, Asta, she says. *Pay* attention.

"How did the fire start?" Dr. Matt is almost eager, the pain of her grasp so tight, so intent, I try to pull away. But she holds me there, pins me down with her burning eyes and her heavy scent and her impossibly powerful touch.

"I don't know," I whisper. Do I?

She exhales a long breath, almost too long for a human being to manage, like she's releasing something I don't understand. Again I get the impression she's a façade, that the woman in front of me is no ordinary person, but hides her true nature behind the mask she wears. It's a crazy thought, but so am I.

"You do know," she says. "Because *you started it.*"

Asta, Zia says.

I barely hear her. My entire being locks up at the accusation. Denial is a physical thing, a fist clenching around me as tight as the grip Dr. Matt has on my arm. It smothers me, suffocating my soul, drowning me in a thick ooze I finally struggle against.

Not true, my heart whispers. Pushing me up through the black, to the surface again. I gasp an inhale and speak. "Not true."

Dr. Matt is closer now, that overpowering taint of fire and sulfur and metal making me gag. "This is the point," she says, "where you always break, Asta. Facing the truth." She won't let me go though I'm struggling, fighting her grasp, twisting my arm to make her release me. I feel my skin tearing under her nails, the bruises she's embedding down to the bone but I can't stop, won't stop. Even as she leans in and whispers in my ear. "*You* started the fire, Asta. And killed your own father."

The chair beneath me clatters as it hits the floor, my wrist aching, my whole body shaking. I finally managed to break away, clutching my arm to my stomach to protect it as it throbs. But what am I really trying to protect?

You need to pay attention, Zia says.

To what? To the fact that I was responsible for Dad dying?

There's more to this, she says. *Asta, if you're ever going to be free, please. Please.*

I stare at Dr. Matt who has retreated back to her normal kindly manner, standing to face me but not trying to touch me.

"This is what you've never been able to accept," the psychiatrist says. "Every time we reach this point, you can't get past it. It's the reason for your psychosis, Asta, for your continuing trauma. If you can just accept that you're responsible for your father's death, I know you can finally be free." She doesn't try to touch me or come closer but I feel her looming over me, pushing against me, dominating me with her words and her energy while I huddle over my hurt wrist and try not to hyperventilate. "The only way to heal is to embrace what you've done, my dear."

It can't be true. I pant that at Zia.

The details are irrelevant, she says, sounding distracted. *You need to see past what she's saying. Because she's not wrong. There's a cycle here that you keep reliving and will continue to relive in this lifetime until you can break it.*

That's cold, cold and horrible, and far too much for me to bear. *You think I did it, too,* I say.

I don't care if you did, Zia says with sharp intent. *Asta, stop it. We've been through worse, trust me. She's manipulating you. Whatever happened, it doesn't matter anymore. You need to wake up.*

But I'm retreating from her, from Dr. Matt. I feel myself doing it internally, even if I just stand there physically.

"You were trying to make your dragon friend breathe fire," Dr. Matt says, kindliness not helping even a little. "You were fascinated by it, even as a little girl. Understandable, considering your beloved father was a hero firefighter." She turns away from me, looking down at the items she's assembled so precisely on the desk. Items I purchased to feed my own delusions. "Your effort lit the whole house ablaze and put you in danger. Danger your father saved you from but couldn't save himself. Asta, it's time to accept what you did."

I can't. I just *can't.* Because no matter what she says, I don't believe a word of it.

"You're *lying,*" I say. That's the worst part. She's probably right. I probably did kill Dad. The irony of not believing it isn't lost on me. And is only feeding the cycle she's already told me I'm in. That I've been living all this time. I'm proof of it, aren't I? That I'll never be free and this prison I'm in? Of drugs and spirals up to joy and then down to oblivion are all on me.

My fault. *My* responsibility.

I could lie back to her. Tell her I accept. I just *can't*. Because I *don't believe her*.

That's the biggest delusion of all. And why I'll never be anything but crazy.

Dr. Matt sighs deeply, another of her impossibly long exhales. For the briefest instant, I see something flicker around her. The image of red scales and flame. I've assigned her an evil persona, I guess, in my mad delusion. Made her a dragon, too. Only one that wants to hurt me.

Hang onto that, Zia says.

While the psychiatrist reaches for the landline phone on the desk.

The orderlies come inside immediately, likely have been waiting in the hallway for just this purpose. I don't fight when I'm injected, accept the gray as it falls over me, heading for dull black and softness.

"We'll try again," Dr. Matt says. "I'll never give up on you, Asta."

And yet, that's exactly what we need her to do, Zia says.

I don't have the capacity to argue with either of them.

CHAPTER EIGHTEEN

It's snowing, giant flakes falling in soft clumps that collect on the window ledge and quiet garden paths outside. I wish the drugs worked. If they would I could forget that it's been a whole year since I met the stranger in the bar, since my life shifted completely toward this trajectory.

Endless days sitting and staring out the window as snow falls.

Christmas came and went without a visit from my mother. I guess I shouldn't be surprised. Dr. Matt's stopped coming, too, the staff psychiatrist encouraging me in group and seeing me once a week, but he's overworked and underpaid and barely has time for even that.

He's easy to lie to. Smiles and nods but won't increase my dosages even when I tell him I can't sleep. That I'm hearing voices.

"You're a model patient," he says, patting my hand and sending me back to the common room to sit and stare into the snow. "You're going to be all right, Ana-*stay-ja*."

I hate it here. It's worse now that I can't find the soft gray. It left me almost immediately after Dr. Matt told me what I can't seem to accept. Zia lingers, too, though she's quiet most of the time. Partly because I keep telling her to shut up, I guess. And despite the fact she said once she can't keep burning me up to keep me with her, that was a lie, too, because here I am.

Aware and awake and wishing for anything but.

I'm sick of listening to her. I'm sick of being crazy. But when I think about finding a way to just go, to just end it, I'm too chicken.

Turns out I'm not even capable of that. Way to be a total and utter loser, Asta. Looks like misery and failure are going to be it for me, then.

When you're done wallowing, Zia says, *I'll be here.*

I shift in my seat, uncomfortable. The impulse to get up and walk around isn't mine, I know. Zia tricks me into getting exercise. It has to be here because if it were up to me, I'd never move, never leave this spot.

You're not real, I say for what has to be the millionth time.

Blah, blah, blah, she shoots back at me. *You're sick? I'm sick, sick and tired of the poor me attitude.* This is the most she's spoken to me in what feels like weeks. *You've had sufficient time to feel sorry for yourself. Can we please finally do something about this?*

You're not very nice to me, I say, hunkering down under my blanket. *You should be. I'm not well.*

You're an idiot, she snaps, unrelenting in her criticism. *I can't believe you're wasting all this time when you could be...*

Could be what? I'm talking to myself again but at least I'm engaging, right?

You could be with El, she says. In a tone that makes my heart ache.

He's not real. I wish he was.

If I could smack you, I would. She's angry again.

Go ahead, I say. *Punish the crazy girl for being broken. You wouldn't be the first one.*

You're pathetic, she says with disgust making my stomach turn over. *Fine. It's the end. What a waste. All those lives, all that time, thrown away by a petulant child who forgot who she really was.* She's on fire, I'm on fire, and her rage is an inferno that makes me cry out in a soft protest. *Goodbye, Anastasia who isn't worthy of the name.*

And then she's gone, just like that, leaving me alone in my head.

Wait. Please, wait. I sit up abruptly, crying out to her. *Come back. Don't leave me alone!*

No reply. No hint, no inkling. Just... nothing.

I sink back into the seat again, panic clutching at my heart, making me tremble. What did I do? The thought crosses that perhaps I've healed. I've finally discarded the trauma by expelling her from my mind.

Except it doesn't feel like that.

For the first time... I feel like I've failed. Lost something I'll never forgive myself for losing. And I weep into my hands while the snow falls.

A hand touches my shoulder and I look up. The orderly flinches back, still afraid of me, his dark eyes only meeting mine for a moment. I remember him and what he tried to do. She terrified him. What will I do without her?

"Your mother is here," he says, backing away. I'm so surprised by the visit that I snuffle and wipe at my face with the blanket as Mom appears. She's lost weight, not that she was ever anything other than a little plump, her hairdo fresh, her nails sparkling with designs. There's a fragility to her, though, that makes me sad as she tugs at the hem of her expensive new coat and doesn't meet my eyes.

"We're leaving," she says to me in a quick, anxious voice. "Let's go."

Leaving? I stare at her, stunned, knowing my mouth hangs open. Where are we going? Mom doesn't say anything, though she glances around like she's anticipating trouble, one hand reaching out toward me. But not to touch me. She snaps her fingers. "Now, Asta. Hurry up."

The next few minutes are a whirlwind while I return to my room and dress in the clothes they hand me, the clothes I came in wearing. They bag off me because I've lost weight, too. Mom speaks low and harshly to the psychiatrist who looks concerned but she's shaking her head with her face tight and her shoulders stiff and then I'm being rushed out the door and into her car.

The back seat of her car, though, not the passenger's seat.

What is going on?

She slams the door on me and climbs into the driver's side and pulls away fast enough that she has to swerve to avoid hitting another car as she jerks the wheel and accelerates out onto the road.

"Mom," I manage at last. "What's going on?"

She shakes her head, her eyes narrowed in the rearview mirror. "This has all been a giant waste of time," she says. "You're not fixed, are you?" I don't know what to say to that. "I've been paying and paying and trying and doing everything and you're still broken." She sounds anxious, almost desperate as she drives too fast, far too fast, down the narrow street and onto the highway. I catch my breath and hold on, the seatbelt digging into my shoulder when she honks her horn and jerks the wheel again, speeding into the far left lane past angry drivers. I see one man give us the finger, his furious expression flashing past me on the way by. "I'm done, Asta," she says. "*We're* done."

What does that even mean? I don't get to ask because she's still talking.

"I moved in with Clyde," she says in a quick blurt that ends in a wavering smile I catch the edges of in the mirror. She flashes her left hand at me over the back of the seat. "He asked me to marry him, Asta." Why does it hurt to hear her desperation when she says it? "A guy like him—a chance like this—doesn't come around often. I have to take it."

"That's great, Mom," I murmur, not sure what else to say.

"It *is* great," she says far too loudly, with fury in her voice. "It's the best thing that ever happened to me." Mom slams one hand down on the steering wheel, still driving far too fast. "I knew you'd see it my way." She turns into traffic, cutting off the car next to her, taking the off-ramp at the kind of speed that forces her to slam on the brakes. I catch myself with both hands, leaning into the seatbelt and the horror of whatever it is that she's doing because I still have no idea. "I deserve a life of my own," she mutters then, turning down a street. She pulls up in front of a house and parks abruptly, breathing hard into the heated air of the car's interior. Her eyes meet mine through the mirror as she makes no move to get out or turn off the engine. "It's *my* time now, Asta. I knew you'd understand."

Someone opens the door next to me and I'm looking up at a woman with frizzy brown hair and crinkle lines around her brown eyes, her hands unbuckling my seatbelt and guiding me up and out of the car. And then I'm standing on the snowy sidewalk, lost and confused as Mom speaks out her open window.

"You're sure this is covered?" Her tone is sharp and anxious still.

"Of course," the woman says. "You still have power of attorney, though, so I'll need your signature on —"

"I'll do it digitally." Mom hesitates one more second, barely turning her head to look at me. "Take care of her." Her window hums as she winds it up and she drives away, her taillights disappearing into the snow while I shiver and watch her go, cold for the first time in a very long time.

Where did the burning inside me go?

"I know this is a lot, Ana-*stay-ja.*" I turn to meet the woman's eyes. She's shorter than me, rather round, but her face is kind and her hands are gentle as she guides me up the path to the house. My gaze roves over the big sign on the lawn, Bay Street Halfway House barely registering as I climb the front steps at her side. "Your mother is right. This is the very best place for you.

"Ana-*staa-zia*," I whisper.

She blinks at me, then nods. "Anastasia." She makes an effort to pronounce it right. "I'm Helen Shriver and this is my care home."

My knees want to buckle. Because while I knew, of course, I knew, I only now let myself know.

Mom abandoned me at last. For Clyde.

Just like that, I'm truly alone.

CHAPTER NINETEEN

Helen shows me to my room after helping me with my boots and coat. The house smells of cooking food and cleaner, though the mix isn't entirely unpleasant, the soft sound of people moving around quietly using murmuring voices in rooms I can't see into carrying me up the carpeted steps. My hand runs over the wooden banister, the old surface shiny. With how many touches just like mine to give it that glow? The world is surreal and I'm in a dream I can't break out of as Helen leads me down the narrow, dim hallway to a wooden door.

"Here we are," she says, gesturing to the metal slots attached with tiny screws. There are paper placards there, three of them, with names my eyes skim over. The bottom one says *Anastasia Fenimore* in carefully printed letters. "I hope you'll be comfortable here with us while you're transitioning."

I don't know what that means. But she seems to think I do as she pushes open the door and waits for me to go inside.

Three beds have been tucked into the corners of the room, two of them already made, with personal items on the shelves around them. The third has sheets and a comforter piled on the end, a pair of new pillows in plastic resting on the floor.

"I thought you might like to make your own bed," Helen says. "To get a feel for normalcy again."

What is going on? I turn to her, shake my head, lost. "I need to go back to the hospital," I say.

She seems surprised by that, slightly alarmed. "Your mother said you've been released," she says. "You're ready for your next step." Helen draws a slow breath. "Is she wrong?"

Mom knows I'm broken. What was she thinking? I look around the room and understand at last. She's dumped me here. Lied to get me out of the facility and left me to fend for myself. Sink or swim. Not her responsibility anymore. Cut me off. Without money or resources.

I should be terrified. Instead, I exhale and clutch my hands to my heart before offering Helen a little smile.

"No," I say. "I'm sorry. I'm just..."

Helen pats my shoulder with a caring nod. "I

understand," she says. "You have a month to get it sorted out, Anastasia. We're here to make sure you do." She turns, gesturing at the trunk at the foot of the bed. "Your mother left you some personal items you can keep there," she says, "but the rest of the boxes are in the basement in your locker. Here's the combination to your lock." She hands me a slip of paper. "When you're ready, I'll introduce you to your roommates. Dinner is in an hour, dear. Is that enough time?"

I have no idea but nod agreeably, because what else am I supposed to do?

"The bathroom is across the hall," she says. "You can use the products in the shower until you get your own. Grocery run is in the morning, so feel free to use whatever you need until then." I don't have any money. Panic returns but she just carries on like I'm not in a weird, foreign world right now that makes no sense at all. "I'll see you downstairs when you're ready." My host then turns and leaves, closing the door softly behind her.

Now what?

I sink to the bed, not because I want to sit but because my knees won't hold me any longer. My hands puddle in my lap, the slip of paper with my locker combination resting there. I stare out the window into the falling snow, unable to move, to function, for a long time.

Are you there? I reach out to Zia. *I can't do this alone.*

No response. Of all the times for my imaginary friend to abandon me. That makes me snort a little laugh that turns into a giggle and then I'm laughing silently, lying on my side on the mattress, hugging myself until the hilarity turns to tears.

It takes a bit longer for the weeping to subside, but when I sit up, I actually feel better. I even make my bed, though it takes me longer than it should since I'm wrung out. I retreat to the bathroom and wash my face, brush my teeth with the new toothbrush in the plastic sleeve that has my name on it, creeping around the space like someone who doesn't belong.

I stand at the top of the stairs, listening to the sounds of voices below, of movement and life going on in the rest of the house, while I try to summon the courage to go down and join them.

Someone knocks on the front door, heavy and hard. I retreat. I couldn't say why or what drives me to duck, to hide from whoever it is that comes to demand attention. I might be insane, but my intuition pushes me hard until I'm crouching behind the railing, breathing heavily out of my mouth and listening as Helen answers the pounding summons.

"Dr. Melusine Matt," her familiar voice says. The psychiatrist is angry. She wasn't part of Mom's recent plan, then. Her words are heavy, fall like weapons in the front entry, her name a threat. "I'm here to see my patient."

Why am I terrified that she's here? That my host will turn me over to her without a fight?

"I'm sorry," Helen says in a crisp tone. "Who are you referring to?"

"Anastasia Fenimore," Dr. Matt says, clipped and

confrontational. "Her mother removed her from care without clearing it with me. The girl is not in any state to be released. She must be returned to the facility for further treatment."

Helen doesn't hesitate. "Even if I could release the names of those in my residence," she says coldly, "only those with authorization are permitted to have any interaction with those who live here."

"Asta is my *patient*," Dr. Matt snarls. I can't see her with my eyes but I can feel her frustration, the influence of her dominant accent surfacing. There's probably fire in her amber gaze.

I shouldn't be shivering. The woman who runs this house is not intimidated by the likes of Dr. Matt. "Clearly, that's not the case," Helen says. "If she were, you'd have been granted access. Instead, it seems, you're mistaken. Now, if you'll excuse me, Dr. Matt, is it? You're on my property illegally and I'd hate to have to call the police to have you removed."

There's a long, terrible silence while I ball my fists against my mouth and try not to sob. Why am I so terrified? I should go down and allow Dr. Matt to return me to the hospital. Mom's choice to pull me out isn't doing me any favors. And the psychiatrist has been my doctor since I was a child. She cares about me, wants to help me, to fix me. Mom just wants to be free of me.

So why then am I so afraid of the woman who's come to take me away?

"Tell Asta I'll be back," Dr. Matt growls before I hear footfalls retreat. The door closes firmly, not quite slamming on her. I huddle where I am, hugging myself, as the soft pad of feet approaches up the steps.

"It's all right, dear," Helen's voice says very softly. I turn my head and meet her eyes through the slats of the banister. Her kindness reminds me of the one who just left. Except I realize there's no agenda in Helen's gaze. Was there always one in the psychiatrist's? "I've dealt with her kind before. Your mother says your doctor isn't allowed to visit. I'll make sure she never sets foot in this house or comes near you for as long as you're in my care." There's such fierce determination in her assurance, I believe her.

"Thank you," I manage to say. "I don't think she cares about me." Why would I tell Helen that?

"Dinner is ready," Helen says then, not responding to my confession, though she seems even more kindly past her fading stubbornness. "Come meet everyone."

It takes a great effort to get off the floor, to descend the stairs. I have to clutch at the railing to hold me up, but I make it and count it a victory that I do. At the bottom, I turn right when instructed, though Helen's direction isn't necessary because the dining room is now filled with women who look up at me as I enter.

"Everyone, this is Anastasia," Helen says. "Let's eat!"

I know I won't remember their names, the women who sit around me at the table, though there's a Chrissy with short hair and a Juliette who has a lot of tattoos, the four others seemingly nice enough, too. I dutifully pass the potatoes and green beans and help myself to roast chicken and homemade bread while they talk and interact and I do my best to stay quiet and unnoticed.

"It's your first night," Helen says when dinner wraps up, "so you're exempt from chores." The other women make faces and unhappy protests, but she just smiles. "I'll show you to the basement and your things, Anastasia."

I hate that they're unhappy, but Helen just eye rolls at me when she leads me to the back of the house, past the kitchen where the women gather to wash dishes and listen to music, chatter filling the space.

"They were all you once," she says, opening a door and turning on the light via the long string with the round, wooden ball on the end, the wavering bulb overhead flickering once before casting a warm, yellow glow over the spare, wooden steps. I follow her into the dank dimness below, two more exposed lightbulbs giving just enough illumination to make the brick-walled basement creepy. "Trust me, you'll fit right in. There," Helen points at the row of what looks like reclaimed school lockers against the far wall under a boarded-up window. "You're number six." She nods to me. "Do you have your combination?"

I fish the slip of paper out of my front pocket where I tucked it away and cross to the battered green door, turning the brand-new lock's round dial until it clicks. When Helen sees that it's worked, she smiles and heads for the stairs.

"Take your time," she says. "Anastasia, you're very welcome here." And leaves me to it.

Why does her simple kindness bring tears to my eyes?

There's not much inside. Three boxes are stacked on top of one another, jammed tightly into the narrow opening. Another sits on the top shelf. I open it first and feel my eyes burn. It's the box with Dad's things in it, the memory box I kept tucked away in my closet. I close it quickly and set it aside, prying the first cardboard box out of the locker, the sharp metal edges making tracks in the softer surface. ASTA is scrawled across the folded flaps, the sticky tape coming loose at the corner. I poke through the barely-folded underwear, socks, t-shirts and pajama pants before closing it up and reaching for the second one.

Jeans, sweaters, random items. A half-empty shampoo bottle and my old brush rattle around on the bottom along with a zippered plastic kitchen bag with old mascara, lip gloss and eyeliner. These are treasures, though, along with half of a tube of toothpaste. Because they belong to me.

So little ever has.

The last box is heavier than it looks, and I'm shocked when I pull out the winter coat and boots to find my journal resting on top of my laptop at the bottom. I guess I assumed Dr. Matt kept possession of the first and Mom just sold it or kept the latter. My fingers are shaking when I lift the journal free. The top right star is gone, the sticker missing, but the pages are intact and however Mom managed to get it back from Dr. Matt, I don't care.

Even if the letter is missing—which it is—it's still

precious. I hug the book to my chest and fight more tears.

More so when I open the lid of my laptop and turn it on. No luck. The battery is dead. But the cable is there and I find an outlet that hopefully won't short out my computer, plugging it in and almost crying out in joy when the device immediately boots up.

It's just a laptop. But it's a lifeline, one I never expected to find.

My book is gone. The file's been wiped clean. Even that doesn't break my heart the way it should. I huddle over the glowing screen, a world of possibilities and hope staring back at me from the pale pink sparkly background I'd adopted for some reason. Covered in stars.

When I've finished packing back up what I don't need and carry away what I choose for the next few days, the journal and laptop are on the top of the pile.

CHAPTER TWENTY

It turns out Mom didn't completely abandon me, at least, not financially. According to Helen, there's enough money in the account my mother set up to fund my exit from her life to keep me here for a month. Though I'm surprised when I mention to my host when she shows me the account amount that I don't know how I'm going to pay for my meds.

"There are no meds here," Helen says. "That's one of the rules, Asta." I've suggested the change in name to the more familiar short version and she's taken it on, as have the rest of the residents. "No drugs in my house. If you still need them, you have to go somewhere else."

Well, I'm still crazy but I've never wanted the meds, so I can live with that.

"Her daughter died," Chrissy tells me. The frizzy blonde with the oversized lips and giant, bulging eyes is one of my roommates. She and Roslyn, a tiny girl with the darkest skin I've ever seen whisper to me at night, holding no grudges despite my fears. "That's why no drugs in the house. Helen blames the doctors for killing her kid."

"We're all nuts anyway," Roslyn says with a little laugh. "Medicating us doesn't change a thing."

I laugh with them. They're not wrong. But I need a plan, it seems, and I'll have to manage it alone. Crazy or not, Zia isn't coming back. Why do I miss her so much?

Because like it or not, she's the only one who's been there for me. My imaginary friend. Inside my head, a figment of my fantasy or not, Zia has at least tried to keep me from falling apart all together.

That makes me think long and hard in the days that pass. And accept that while yes, hearing her voice means I was—and am—crazy, at least I had someone.

Someone I now miss more than I can express. It's funny to me that I finally move on because I know she'd want me to. As nuts as that is, it's the memory of Zia fighting for me that makes anything I do from that point on even remotely possible.

I just wish she hadn't left me, even if that means I'll never be healed.

It also means this is new, all of it, and uncomfortable. I'm restless without the endless depressing wallowing, I find, and am immediately put to work when Helen sees I'm in need. I've never enjoyed cleaning per se but there's a great satisfaction in polishing all the wood in the old house, in sweeping and scrubbing the floors, in cleaning the bathtubs and toilets that surprises me.

"My sister Janet has a cleaning business," Helen says to me on the fourth day. "She's always looking for girls."

"Crazy girls?" I grin at Helen, amused.

She laughs. "Those are the best kind," she says. "I've already told her about you, Asta. If you want a job, it's yours."

I fall into a rhythm in the house, one that feels safe and has happy moments I wasn't expecting. And yet, this place feels like a cocoon, like I've wrapped myself up with these women I barely know, all protected by the careful, kind and wonderful energy of Helen Shriver.

I know it's a trap as much as the hospital. It's not hard to accept or acknowledge that I could easily fall into a lifetime here, volunteering to help her, making a life for myself. I'm working for Helen's lovely sister Janet in her cleaning business, the pair carbon copies of one another despite five years between them, with the same sense of humor and kindness to spare. I'm doing nothing at all past the confines of this oasis of existence that my mother gifted me.

It's hard to be grateful to Mom for much but honestly? If she knew that she'd saved me in her need to cut me loose, I don't think she'd believe it for a second.

It's almost a week before I start writing again. My first day cleaning with Janet has triggered something I wasn't planning on. Being outside the house, in someone else's space, in a big, lovely place with pictures of laughing children and a happy couple has me longing for more despite myself.

I won't ever find it. I'm too broken for that kind of future. And maybe being lured out of the web of protection that is Helen's house is a mistake, but I know I can't stay. When sleep refuses to come, the story surfaces as I struggle to rest. My laptop chugs briefly when I open it, descent to the dining room just past midnight, quiet and solitary.

I never thought I'd write again. But when I rest my fingertips on the keyboard and inhale, words pour out. Words that aren't mine, I swear it, but are, fed through me by something, someone I can't control or begin to understand.

Not the book I wrote before, though. A different one. It surfaces like the woman who tells it to me has been waiting for me to hurry back and get to her at last. Her turn.

Morning shines through the window over my screen before I blink and sit back. Helen is standing in the doorway of the dining room, a faint smile on her face.

"Coffee?"

I smile back, dazed and suddenly very, very happy. "I'll make it," I say.

She shakes her head, winking. "I have a feeling you

need it more than I do."

I put the laptop away after triple-checking that I've saved the new document. It's a totally different story, in the series, yes, but many lives ahead, in Victorian London. But there's no doubt in my mind it's the same characters, the girl and her dragon, a new life she's living with him and though it's proof I'm still a crazy girl, I'm okay with it.

Those are the best kind, Helen's voice reminds me.

It's almost dinner and I'm helping peel potatoes when someone knocks on the door. Helen goes to answer, as always. She doesn't let us, just in case. But I peek out into the hallway anyway, not alone, either, the gathering of women nosy as to who this newcomer might be. I'm shocked to see a face I know and I'm already moving before Helen can send him away.

"Jared." I stop a few feet from the open door. Helen turns to frown at me, but Jared is holding something out and I'm reaching for it, a thick envelope that's heavy in my hand before he speaks.

"I thought you should have that back," he says. Before turning and hurrying away.

Helen closes the door, one eyebrow arched at me. "You know the rules," she says, but she's gentle. "Do you want me to look?"

I shake my head, hands trembling. I already know what it is. When I tear open the envelope, the stack of pages makes my vision waver as my eyes burn. I smile at her, beaming, because Mom isn't the only one who gave me a gift.

"It's all right," I say, hugging my book to my chest.

It's more than that. It's a miracle.

Why does it suddenly seem like life is actually working in my favor?

I retreat to my room after dinner, forcing myself to wait. As excruciating as that delay is, it's worth it as I read the top page on the stack, typed out but signed by Jared himself.

I never thought you deserved what they did to you, he wrote. *They said you were nuts, but I never believed it. Your mom and my dad are getting married. I guess that means you're my sister.* There are layers of creepy there that make me wince but I read on anyway. *I'm sorry I turned you in that time. I guess this makes us even. Jared.*

I set aside the letter and stare down at the title page. *Dragon Girl* by Anastasia Fenimore stares back at me.

I'm terrified and excited at the same time. Do I dare read what I wrote? Will it trigger me? I've come so far by what feels like utter luck and chance. I can't go back to the hospital. But if I can't face what I made, what brought me here in the first place, can I ever be free?

I will not have that fear hang over me for the rest of my life. With a big inhale, I flip the page. And begin to read.

As it all comes rushing back to me.

I know Chrissy and Roslyn come and go. I get up and retreat to the dining room when they want to go to bed. Hours pass on the outside while a whole lifetime engulfs me on the inside until I'm looking up, the corner lamp my only illumination, the quiet house breathing around me.

My beautiful, delicious delusion. Even if it *is* one, it's *mine*.

I fetch my laptop without hesitation and begin to enter the book into a new file. In an act of utter defiance that leaves me breathless and excited, I reclaim the fantasy, only this time there's no one to stop me from doing it.

Mine.

Forever mine.

But that's not the end. It takes me three days between cleaning shifts and chores around the house, three nights of stolen time, to type the whole thing back into the computer again. And another day to go over it with an online grammar tool to make sure it's not a total mess. On a sunny, chilly Sunday afternoon over a cup of hot chocolate while the other women chat and dream, I build a cover that I compare to those professionals have made, doing my clumsy best to fit in.

And finally, during a breathless morning at the bank where I set up an account in my name and my name only, I create an account that I use to set up my online author profile and then, in a hasty and terrified rush of anxiety, press publish.

I consider using a penname. I don't want them to see what I've done. Not because it will get Jared in trouble, though it's a consideration. It's just... Mom. Dr. Matt. What will they say? What will they do?

And yet, this is mine. No one will take it from me ever again. As the seed of a plan forms and I make a choice.

I show Helen the book, the digital format and paperback I struggle to learn to create, breathlessly anxious. Then share with the ladies in the house. And groan as they all rush to read it, amid cheers and teasing and laughter.

Only to have them come to me while I work on the sequel, one at a time and with tears in their eyes, to hug me and whisper how much they loved it and can they please have the next one...?

That's the first time that I allow myself to believe that maybe, just maybe, I'm not writing these stories only for me. And when I finally check my account, look at the retail sales of that book I wrote and threw out into the world, I can't believe it.

Strangers have bought it. Read it. Reviewed it.

Loved it. And now, I have hope that has nothing to do with the cocoon of this house.

I really *am* free.

CHAPTER TWENTY-ONE

My steps are fast and solid as I climb to the front door, my body the strongest it's ever been, carrying me with purpose and confidence as I reach for the knob. Three months of cleaning has added muscles to my frame that has filled out somewhat thanks to Helen's good food and my own hard work. Is it wrong I take pride in the way feel as I pass through the door and into the front hall of what I've come to call home?

Life might not have turned out the way I thought it should, but I'm not complaining. There's a comfortable safety to this place that's embraced me far past the time I was meant to leave and though I already have plans to go, I'll be sad when I do.

Helen appears at the dining room door, a dishcloth in her hands, a beaming smile on her face. "You're home!" She hurries to my side and hugs me with enthusiasm I return. "How was your day?"

"Great," I say, shucking out of my coat and hanging it in the hall closet, my sneakers tucked away beneath it, tidiness now a compulsion I know I'll never shake. "Janet wants me to head up her new cleaning crew." Helen's sweet, loud and lovely sister made the offer just this afternoon. It's part of the reason I feel so buoyant, of course, though a part of me wonders about accepting the role. Not because I can't handle it. I'm past that worry.

There's something else that I feel like I need to do. I just can't remember what that is.

"She told me," Helen gushes at me. "I'm so proud of you, Asta." I'd never heard anyone say that to me before I met Helen and Janet. I hear it regularly now. Never gets old, though. "You've come so far," she says, dropping her hands, the damp spot on my sleeve left behidn from the wetness of the cloth she holds making goosebumps rise.

Or maybe it's the knock on the door behind me? I shiver, like a premonition of something, though there's no reason to feel that way. Except when knocks come to this door—a door that doesn't open for just anyone—I pay attention.

So does Helen. I turn as her expression tightens, the woman I've come to adore visibly girding herself as though for war. I've learned in the last twelve weeks that the mistress of this house will take no shit from anyone. Not cops come to speak to the accused, not lawyers looking for a quick paycheck. Not exes with axes to grind. Or psychiatrists demanding to speak to old clients... she's the bravest woman I've ever met and I only hope that one day I can return the gift she's given me.

The courage and encouragement to be myself without apology.

Normally, I'd leave and let her deal with whoever it is that's knocking. She prefers it that way. But something keeps me in place, won't let me abandon her. I'm past the point of fearing who might come calling anyway. And though my hands ache from the scrubbing and my knuckles are cracking from the gloves I wear to work, I put off going upstairs to soak them and smear them with moisturizer.

Because of Helen Shriver, I'm safe, I'm strong and I have money in the bank account I set up. It's not much, but it's growing every day now that I've paid for the things that need to be taken care of to ensure I stay free.

She deserves to know that she's not alone, either.

Helen glances at me as though wondering why I'm still there before smiling a little and nodding. Does she know why I cross my arms over my chest and nod back? I hope so. I'll defend her against all comers, no matter what the cost. The fierceness of that truth fires me up for no reason and I'm ready for a fight even before I know who it is she has to face.

As if I'm a character in one of the books I write. That makes me grin.

Helen jerks the door open with her expression flat and unwelcoming, like always and while I know better than to expose myself, I lift my chin and stand there beside her at the door.

The goosebumps I felt were a foretelling after all. How did I know it would be Mom staring back at me from the front porch? I don't feel even a flicker of surprise. Her face is pale, her hand shaking as my mother—who I haven't seen in three months, heard from, who cut me off four weeks in—drops her arm to her side, her next knock interrupted. "Asta," she says. Swallows. "Pumpkin."

She's not alone. Dr. Matt stands behind her. I should be afraid of them, tension inside me a familiar feeling that's odder not being present than it ever was dominating me.

Helen glances at me again, frowning. But she's not angry I didn't follow the rules and have exposed myself to those she's there to protect me from. I can see that in the tight irritation on her face. She's worried about me. Of anyone in my life, Helen cares, really cares, and never judges.

It's time for her to see that it's because of her that I really am who I need to be.

"Mom," I say in the same tone Helen always uses with visitors, flat and emotionless. "What do you want?"

Dr. Matt steps forward with that same old gentle smile I no longer trust. Why did I ever trust it, trust her? It's so clear to me now that she has some kind of agenda with her smooth smile and graceful attempt to use my mother as a means to an end. I'm that end. But why? I realize I have no idea why Dr. Matt won't let me go and now I want to know. "Asta," she says, taking over immediately like I've chosen to let her in. "You look well."

"Neither of you are welcome here," Helen says abruptly, about to close the door. Why do I stop her? I need this confrontation, I realize, and gently shake my head at her. She stares back, distress surfacing. "You're sure?"

I nod. "It's all right," I say. Knowing that it really is. I step out into the early spring evening. The wind is still chilly but it's a far cry from the winter that I've endured my entire life so I breathe into it, dry and sore hands in the pockets of my jeans as I face down Mom and Dr. Matt. Helen let me stay long past the month I was supposed to, supported my choice to hire a lawyer, to make decisions for myself. I know she doesn't do it for everyone. I'll find a way to pay her back. But I'll never be able to repay her for what three months in her care has done for me. The confidence its given me. "What can I do for you?"

"We understand you've started writing again," the psychiatrist says.

"Asta, you have to stop." Mom twitches next to Dr. Matt, reaching for me though when I don't pull away—when I don't react at all—she drops her hand again. "Pumpkin, I'm so worried."

"Right," I say. "Worried someone might find out that you dumped your crazy kid and left her to fend for herself." I should be bitter. I'm really not. I'm still grateful, despite everything. Even having her right here in front of me, I can't muster resentment. But I won't tell her that I'm thankful she cut me off.

She doesn't deserve that.

"You gave me no choice." Mom wrings her hands, her gaunt face pinking at the cheekbones, mottled redness climbing down her neck and over her chest. "I did *everything* for you."

"Asta," Dr. Matt intervenes, "this was a last-ditch effort on your mother's part. We've talked it over, however. Haven't we, Caroline?" Mom nods, her misery visible, though without a hint of regret that I can see. "We need you to come back to the hospital, Asta. You're clearly breaking down again. I couldn't bear it if you did so without support."

"I have lots of support," I say in the brightest tone I can muster, even smiling at both of them. But my expression is meant to cut, not soothe, and I know it's working because Mom backs off a step even if Dr. Matt doesn't. "And a life, now. Finally. Funny how that happened after I was free of both of you." I don't allow them to respond, accepting the hurt on Mom's face. "So, if you'll excuse me, I decline your invitation." I look back and forth between them. "Was there anything else?"

"Don't make me call the police," Mom says. Her attempted threat makes me grin. Because I saw this coming. It's so satisfying to be able to settle into my sense of strength. The reason I don't have more cash in my account, why I'm here at Helen's longer than most? I put all of my money toward this very contingency with Helen's help and approval. The reason I'm only now able to stockpile money from the job I've been slaving over relentlessly.

"I take it the paperwork hasn't made it to your new address," I say. "From my lawyer." Mom flinches, looks at Dr. Matt whose face doesn't change expression. "I've had your power of attorney revoked, Mom. It took a bit of work, and a state psychiatrist to sign off. But I did it. With money *I* earned." Now my anger finally surfaces as I tap my chest with my index finger. "*My* money, not yours. You can keep your guilt and your payoff and you can leave. Now."

They both stare at me, Mom clearly waiting for Dr. Matt to do something. When the psychiatrist finally nods, my mother seems shocked.

"Congratulations," Dr. Matt says in a soft, sad voice. "I'll be here when you fall apart again, Asta." She reaches out before I can stop her and grasps my wrist. I flinch from the contact, because it's the same wrist she bruised, that memory surfacing, the same one she cut with those long, dark coffin nails. Something tingles between us and I jerk my hand away before I can stop myself. "I'll be seeing you soon, dear. Let's go, Caroline."

Dr. Matt turns and walks away, not waiting to see if Mom follows or not. My mother stares at me for a long moment, lips opening and closing, no sound emerging. And then she spins and hurries after the psychiatrist in a lurching and almost mechanical way that has me hugging myself.

Is it over? Or is Dr. Matt right?

"Come inside, Asta," Helen's voice says from behind me. I turn to find she's waiting just past the door. She clearly heard the whole conversation, her glare fixed on the black sedan Dr. Matt drives away with Mom's pale face staring out the passenger's window.

"I'm sorry about that—" I choke off my words when Helen embraces me, holding me tight in the quiet front hall of her house that hugs me, too.

"I'm so proud of you," she says and it's the best thing ever, hoarse and soft. Then pulls away, blinking tears with a big smile. "Now, go shower. You smell like you've been working all day."

I laugh.

It feels amazing.

—fire blazes, engulfing me, the sound of screaming around me, as a hand reaches through the flames, diamond glinting in the blaze—

I jerk awake, disoriented and shaking. My fingers hurt. I look down at my hand, at the match in my grasp, the end of it against my skin, ember flaring before it goes out.

The twisted black remnants shatter as the used-up match hits the floor, panic a knot in my chest I can't breathe around.

How did I get here? I'm sleepwalking again. The last time, I ended up outside. I don't ever remember doing anything like this—

—fire and flame and my dad—

No. I quickly rip a paper towel from the roll on the counter and wet it in the sink, soaking up the charred remains of the match, scrubbing where it fell though there's no mark there to clean. When I finally toss the remains into the trash and close the door, I'm still shaking.

I can't stop shaking.

Nor can I sleep. I lie there with the blankets pulled up tight to my neck, the sound of my newest roommates breathing in the other beds doing nothing to slow the panic roll that unfolds like a dark and deadly flower in my head.

What if I had set fire to the house? What if I killed everyone?

I didn't. Nothing happened. This time. But it's impossible not to spiral down into the center of that blossom of guilt, despair and dread. *Was* Dr. Matt right? Am I just a timebomb ticking and ticking my way down to ruining everything?

There's no way I'm telling Helen. I can't risk it. She'll kick me out, I'm positive of that. I have no one to talk to, to confide in. Which means I throw myself into work instead, taking on extra jobs, writing when I'm not, so I don't have to think. Wearing out my body and my mind so I won't sleepwalk again.

I wait until the others are asleep every night before tying myself to the heavy metal frame of my bed with a scarf, on the far side against the wall so they won't see. Just in case.

That's a mad thing to do, I know it is. But I just need a little longer. To get out on my own. To have enough rent to pay for an apartment. Then what, though? So I can burn down a different building? I fight panic regularly, so much so it becomes a constant companion that makes me long for meds.

I wake a week later tugging at the scarf on my wrist and I know I need to do something. I can't risk everyone at Helen's. I have to go now, not later. I've been putting it off for too long. The only apartment I can afford is crappy and gross and means three busses to get to work, but it'll be worth it not to risk Helen and her house.

She cries when I tell her, but she's happy, proud of me. There is no way I'm telling her why I'm really leaving. I hug her, go to my room, pack my few things into the boxes my mother left me, most of my old life already recycled to others so I don't have to be reminded of who I used to be.

As I sit on the end of the bed, my last night in this refuge, I do something I didn't plan to do. I open my email and type in an address I can't seem to forget.

helios@eliosveles.com.

I know you're not real, I type. *That this will just end up in my own inbox. But I want you to know I still think about you. You're the reason I'm free. Love, Asta.*

I stare at the message for a long moment before hitting send. The click of the laptop lid closing makes me sigh.

—fire, flames all around me, voices screaming, his hand is strong and I take it—

I'm coughing when I wake, heavy smoke filling the room. I'm on my feet, standing in the middle of the wooden floor in my pajamas.

While the dream and reality mingle as someone starts to scream.

The someone is me.

CHAPTER TWENTY-TWO

The house is on fire? It can't be. Is it my fault? I should be panicking but the initial scream dies as I lunge for the bed next to me. The woman in it has barely been with us for a day, Mary or Marie or something like that. I don't bother with names, jerking her out of bed and sending her toward the door as I help the other woman, Jada, while she tries to gather her things.

"Out!" I shout that in her face. "Now!"

She bolts, following our other roommate, and I exhale into the smoke in relief because I forgot to check the door handle. But wherever the fire has started it's not outside the room. More voices join in, a chorus of women startled and afraid and then scrambling for the stairs. I stay at the top, funneling them down to the first floor, arm over my mouth and nose, squinting into the heavy smoke that's thickening as it billows up from wherever the fire began.

Helen appears at my side, terrified but as solid as ever, pushing me toward the steps. I make her go first the pair of us exchanging a look before we separate and check each bedroom for anyone who might have been missed.

The young woman has wedged herself under the bed, panting in hysterical fear, forcing me to grab her ankles and pull her out with a violent jerk that will no doubt leave a mark. But she's clutching at me, her breath on my face, and I'm lifting her and carrying her to the doorway where Helen takes her and carries her to the top of the staircase.

As fire finally erupts through the wall near the back of the house and drives me toward the first floor with its heat.

I'm stumbling down the steps, my bare feet sliding over the carpet that quickly crisps in the intensity of the flames now writhing and chuckling their way down the hallway, the roaring rush of a freight-train of devouring light and heat pushing me forward with a rush of air so hot it has its own identity.

Helen is on the front porch, yelling at the women to keep retreating, and I'm almost to her when I hear it—the thin wail of a voice behind me. It's almost lost in the roar of the fire, in the sharp oncoming scream of a fire engine's siren. I spin without thinking, throwing myself back into the house, Helen yelling my name.

"Asta!"

The air is heavy, almost like a weight above me, and I'm forced to crouch, to crawl, into the kitchen. There's no light, I can't see, let alone breathe, but I still hear it. The wail, thin and terrified. It wakes a memory in me, and then I'm—

—*surrounded by fire, women in white dresses, their hair bursting into flame, melting around their faces, as they fall and stumble over one another, trying to run when there's nowhere to go*—

—*as a giant amber eye blinks open right in front of me, the slit of a pupil contracting into a black line as tall as I am, huffing sound of fresh flame making the fire sway*—

I stumble over something and grab for it, hands clutching at a bare leg, feel whoever it is clutching back. And then we're sliding over the hot linoleum and onto wood and somehow I'm rolling out the front door with the weight of another person in my arms, tumbling down onto the walkway, with hands pulling at me, jerking me free of the path as large bodies in heavy suits, with masks and hoses and axes rush past.

I'm sobbing. Coughing and choking.

"Asta." Helen hugs me around my neck and I can't breathe again, but for the right reason. "You saved us."

I want to tell her I fear she's wrong, that this is on me. But I don't. Instead, I lay there in her arms and watch her whole world burn.

When the police approach, I'm not surprised. Dr. Matt's with them, of course, she is. Pointing at me, telling them something. I hand back the oxygen mask the EMT pressed into my hands and meet Helen's eyes as the two detectives grimly gesture for me to stand up.

"I didn't," I say. "What they're going to tell you I did." Why do I protest when I'm not sure?

Because you didn't. Wait, Zia? The sound of her voice makes my heart soar and I writhe inside with the need to scream her name. *This wasn't you, Asta.*

Helen stares back. "I know," she says. Glares at the cops. "This woman is a hero. Don't you *dare*."

Her faith means more than she'll ever know. But it's having Zia back that straightens my spine, stiffens my resolve. Convinces me that, no matter what anyone says, I'm innocent, damn it all.

Because Zia says so.

"Asta," Dr. Matt says, "has a history with fire. Detectives?"

They lead me away. I don't fight them. I'm not even afraid. I let everyone stare, not like I can stop them. The cops don't cuff me, though. There's that much. But I do get a ride to the station in the back of a cruiser.

I take that time to reach out to the voice in my head I missed way more than I should have for a woman who wants to be seen as sane. *ZIA!*

I'm here, she says. *I've got you, Asta.* She sounds the same as always, if a little sad. *I'm sorry.*

I'm not. I remember the sensation of her hugging me in the hospital and wrap my arms around myself while picturing doing the same to her. I have an image of her in my mind, though I have no clue where it came from. I use every ounce of my energy to hug her, too. Because I'm crazy, yes, and I'm so very happy she's back.

It's going to be okay, she says. *I need you to stay quiet. Don't say a word to the police. Can you do that?* She sounds like she's ready to argue.

Yes, I say. *Anything you want. Just don't leave me again.* I keep that private, or try to. If she hears me, she doesn't comment.

I'm way happier than I should be when we pull up to the police station.

They don't officially book me. I sit in a room with a one-way mirror, feeling like I'm in some kind of TV show, staring at the bottle of water they gave me, coughing occasionally, the stink of smoke as painful as the tiny char marks on my skin. Pinpricks the fire left behind. I'm lucky, so lucky. I should be dead.

But it's not my fault.

It's not, Zia says.

Oh, good, I laugh at her, my mood still far too light for the situation I'm in. *My imaginary friend agrees with me. That's comforting.*

She snorts. It almost makes me grin.

I shouldn't have left you, she says.

I didn't give you reason to stay, I say. *I'm sorry.* Am I really having this conversation with someone who doesn't exist? She's real to me, though. That's what matters. More real than a lot of people in my life.

I can only be here and help you if you want me to be. She sounds frustrated. *It's complicated. And I can't tell you everything. Trust me, I wish I could.* She hesitates then. *Even I have gaps.* She exhales softly. *We need to find him, Asta. As soon as we're out of here, we need to find El.*

Of course, if that's what she says. I don't question her even though I want to ask why, what the gaps are, who he is to us. But I don't get the chance. The door to the interview room opens and the grim detectives enter. Not to question me or even officially arrest me, though. Instead, they gesture for me to rise, the woman offering me her hand.

"We had to be sure," she says. "Your psychiatrist was pretty convincing."

"She's not my psychiatrist," I say as Zia growls the same. So nice to have backup again. "What happened?"

"One of the women was smoking up in the kitchen," the other detective says, gruff and angry. "She passed out, lit the fire by accident. You saved her life. She just confessed."

Not my fault. For real.

Told you, Zia says.

Welcome back to the crazy, I say. And burst into tears.

It takes a few minutes to pull myself together, but I manage it. I even shake the detective's hand. Why am I not surprised to find Dr. Matt waiting for me in the foyer of the station?

"Asta," she says as I push my way past her.

"Leave me alone," I say, gulping fresh air the moment I'm outside. It gives me a buffer against the smoke smell that I didn't realize I needed. I wipe my face with both hands, looking down at myself in my ruined socks and pajamas.

"You weren't responsible," she says. "This time."

"I said," I spin on her, snarling in her face, "leave me *alone*."

And walk away.

Good girl, Zia says. *Makes me wonder, though.*

Wonder what? This is different. Our relationship. There's a deeper connection to her than I've ever felt before, without the drugs, without walls I built. Still, she's thinking about the past and I'm lost in the present. I hesitate on the sidewalk. Where do I go? What do I do? My things are all burned in the house. I want to cry over the loss of my computer. I have money in my account, yes. But there's no one here to help me. No one waiting for me. Helen has her own problems.

I can't wait for someone to rescue me.

Except, I don't need anyone. I have myself. And Zia.

And she has other things for me to consider. *I want to know if this isn't the first time you were blamed for something you didn't do.*

Why does that idea fill me with a sudden shock of fury?

CHAPTER TWENTY-THREE

Helen is standing outside the remains of her house when I arrive. She hugs me, a smudge of ash on her cheek. It's clear she's been weeping, but she's as caring as ever as she links arms with me.

"You saved all of us," she says. "I'll never forget that, Asta."

I guess I really did.

She's found places for all of the women, but I turn her down when she tries to do the same for me.

"It's my turn to help you," I say. "Where will you go?"

Helen's smile is sad but firm. "Janet's," she says. "Until I can sort all of this out." She waves both hands at the house. "You're sure?"

I nod. This was my last night anyway.

My apartment is small, barely a bachelor, but it's mine. I've learned how to clean and pour my whole being into it that first day, spending some of my preciously hoarded money to wipe away the grime and the stink of the previous residents. I'm already determined not to stay long, grimly sweeping away the carcass of a cockroach that I'm firmly evicting from my new home.

You don't need to do this, Zia tells me as I swipe the last of the dust from a window ledge. *El will take care of everything if you let him.*

I trust her, I do. I believe she has my best interest at heart like no one else. Because she's me. But.

I need to do this for myself, I tell her. *For once, I need to know I can.*

She sighs. *We've always been stubborn,* she says. *And independent to a fault. Just don't forget your promise, Asta.*

I won't, I say.

We'll see, she tells me before going quiet. Not gone, just… waiting.

I won't let her down, I swear it. And if I'm going to make it I have to learn to trust myself.

My computer is gone, but I saved everything to the cloud, even if I can't afford to replace it just yet. A cheap used tablet eats up the last of my savings, but it means I can get online at a café where I sip a coffee I nurse so they won't kick me out. After confirming my account is still there, that my work is still safe, I do what Zia suggests I do when I put off the other

request—what I'm afraid to do, despite everything—
and search my father's name.

Why have I never done this before? Because I
thought I knew the truth, of course. I was raised to
believe the story I was told. Lived in trauma and guilt
and never once questioned anything Mom said, that
Dr. Matt insisted was the source of my insanity.

For the first time ever, I read the handful of news
articles archived about the fire.

Should I be surprised it was deemed an accident?
No, of course not. It wasn't like six-year-old me set
the fire on purpose or anything. I force myself to read
every word of every story, starting with the first one.
Hero Firefighter Dies in House Blaze, the headline read.
The photo of my dad makes me teary, but I don't look
away. I know that picture, had that same one in the
box of memories. Smiling with his blue eyes crinkled
at the corners, in his black uniform and hat, in front
of a blue background and a flag.

It takes me a moment to process the initial story.
...died in a house fire saving the life of his daughter...

Yes, I know that much. The next article has Dad's
picture, too, but beside it is a shot from the fire. How
had the reporter gotten inside? It doesn't matter. I
stare at the scene, making the image as big as I can
though it's pixelated when I do.

The kitchen. Where the fire started.

The story repeats a lot of what the first already told
me, ending with a pending investigation claim. That
has me moving on to the final article.

This one has another image, four squares this time,

the one of dad in the top left and the other four of the interior of the house. The reporter's opening headline has me stiffening.

Hero's Death Ruled Accidental, it says. *Investigators in the death of acclaimed Lieutenant David Fenimore announced today that the fire that took his life was an accident caused by a faulty pilot light in the kitchen stove.*

Zia hisses in my head. I barely hear her.

A faulty pilot light.

Keep reading, she says.

I do, barely breathing.

Though the fire claimed his life, Lieutenant Fenimore was a hero to the end, rescuing his own daughter from the blaze before succumbing to his injuries. He is survived by his loving wife, Caroline, who wasn't home at the time of the blaze.

Your mother. Zia's anger burns hotter than any fire I've endured or imagined. *Where was she that night, Asta?*

I… don't know. I never asked.

Look at the pictures. I do. *What's that at the front door?*

It takes me a moment. *Camping gear,* I say. *We were—*

Sorry, kiddo, Dad says as he hangs up the phone. *We'll have to leave in the morning, okay? I have to take care of something.* He carries me to bed, tucks me in. El is snuggled in next to me as Dad goes to my bedroom door and turns out the light. *I'll see you bright and early, okay?*

He leaves it open a crack, just the way I like it—

Asta. Zia's whisper isn't loud but it's enough to bring me back.

I swallow hard. If I don't, I'm going to be sick. *We were supposed to go camping. But Dad got a call, had to do something for one of his friends. We were going to go in the morning.* I can remember suddenly. It's as surprising as anything I've endured that I remember so vividly.

Where was your mother? She asks that again and I don't have an answer. *Look at the other picture, Asta.* I do, the first on the bottom. It's the image from the other article, of the kitchen. *What do you see?*

Nothing, I say. What am I supposed to see?

Now, the last one, Zia says. She's very insistent.

My bedroom. *It's my bedroom.* Wait, what's that on the floor? "El," I whisper, choking on the name.

Elliot the dragon, Zia says, her fury not quite reaching me yet. *In your room. Not in the kitchen at all.*

Where the fire started. Where they said *I* started it. With my toy. Trying to make him breathe fire.

Asta, Zia says. *Where was your mother?*

I sit back abruptly, raising startled looks from some of the people around me and have to force a smile that barely lifts my lips. When I turn toward the street, the picture window, I see the grimace on my face, the rage now surfacing in my own eyes as I stare at myself—at Zia—in our reflection in the glass.

I didn't do it, I say. Relief is a splash of cold that unexpectedly feeds the fire inside me despite the dichotomy.

You did not, she says. *This is proof.*

Why would they lie to me? Why? *Maybe Mom lied to Dr. Matt?*

They would have had the report from the fire inspector, Zia says. *Stop cutting them slack, Asta. They knew.*

They *knew.* I choke on it. Chew it up.

Spit it out.

I'm on my feet and outside before I know I'm moving, my feet carrying me fast and hard down the sidewalk. Is it fate that I'm close enough to Dr. Matt's office that it takes me barely five minutes to reach her door? I doubt it. Zia seems to be satisfied by that truth, so it's likely she's influencing my choices. So be it. Not like I'm unaccustomed to being manipulated.

Hey, she says. *I'm here to help.*

I don't respond. I'm too busy storming through the door and confronting the newest of Dr. Matt's meek little receptionists.

Who barely meeps her protest at me when I push my way past the entry and to the door I know so well. The only thing that stops me is the sound of Dr. Matt's voice, muffled on the other side as I reach for the knob.

"—stay away from her," she's saying as I jerk the door open.

It's icy inside, but that's a good thing, Dr. Matt standing slowly as I cross to her desk. My whole being is on fire and for the first time in my life, I embrace the flames as I confront her with a sneer I can't curtail.

"I didn't kill my dad," I say. "You lied to me. I want to know why."

She sets the phone down without saying goodbye to whoever it was she'd been speaking to. There's fire in her amber eyes—

—a giant, amber eye appears, the pupil's slit contracting—

I gasp a little, sway, as she circles toward me with both hands out.

"Asta," she says. "I'm so glad you're here."

I stagger back, though, the visceral reaction to the vision a clenched fist around me that drives terror into me. "No," I whisper. I don't even know what I'm protesting.

"It's all right," she says in that horrible, gentle, kind voice that's a lie, it's all a lie—

—flames and screaming and women dying as that eye focuses on me—

"You…" I'm dying inside. Zia is calling my name and I'm falling into a pit but I can't stop it, can't stop myself from collapsing into the madness that wants to eat me alive as Dr. Matt tries to touch me. "You—"

"Asta." She grasps my wrist and fire blooms between us. "It's time, dear. To take your meds."

Compulsion is a crushing giant that engulfs me as her gaze draws me out of myself—

ASTA! I jerk free of Dr. Matt, but it wasn't me who pulled away. It was Zia. *Run. Now!*

I do. I spin and flee, hitting the sidewalk at a startling pace, blocks away by the time I pant to a halt in an alley and bend in half, palms pressing to my thighs.

Who… who is she? I'm the crazy one, yes, but what was *that?*

It doesn't matter anymore, Zia says. She's grim, and angry. *I suspected, but… it's going to be okay. Just stay away from her, Asta.*

I lean back against the wall. *What's wrong with me?*

She sighs. *Nothing,* she says. *I'm so sorry. This is my fault. I need you to believe that, okay? There's never been anything wrong with you. But they got to you before I woke up and remembered who we are.* Her anger is tinged with frustration, with grief. *I shouldn't have left you last time. I won't ever again. Not until you remember, too.*

Remember what? I'm all in now, regardless of the outcome.

There's so much to tell you, she says. *But I'm not the one to do it. I don't think I have to, anyway. Check your email, Asta. You should have an answer by now. If one is coming.* Now she's worried.

An answer? To what?

The next café's coffee is terrible, but I don't care because I'm not there for the drink I spend the last of my change on. My hands are shaking as I do as I'm told. There's an anxiety and a hope inside me that I don't understand as I open my email app and check it like she told me to do.

Delusional, yes. But she's not wrong.

Helios@eliosveles.com has replied. And while I'm still on the fence whether I've only answered myself or if this is real after all, I open it anyway.

CHAPTER TWENTY-FOUR

My dearest Anastasia.

I can hear his voice saying the words. And it's not just from memory, from meeting him that one time, either. I remember with a deep ache that haunts me as I read on.

I had no idea she interfered.

Who?

Keep reading, Zia says. Why is my mind now blossoming with joy?

When you didn't respond to my first reply, I thought the message was in error. I know now it was her further attempt to insert herself between us. I will not allow that again. Come to me. And if you can't, I will come to you. I only ask that you tell me one way or another.

Yours always,

El

Zia laughs in my head. I'm giddy and breathless and barely holding it together.

Where? One word at a time. I can manage one word at a time.

Check the attachment, she says.

There's a file? I click it. A flight itinerary pops up. For tonight. On the other side of the country.

This is nuts, I say.

Hey, you're the one who claims to be crazy. Zia laughs again. *We're getting on that plane if I have to knock you senseless and take over.*

She's amused but she's not kidding. This time, I accept.

And I'm terrified. *I need to know what this is.*

I can't tell you, she says, suddenly serious. *You have to see for yourself, Asta.*

First things first. If I am crazy, if I sent myself this email like Dr. Matt claimed I did before, I need to know. But unless I've created an account I can't access from my new-to-me tablet, that much is debunked. As for the flight itinerary, it's for a real ticket. And not one I purchased, either, as I cold sweat my way through a search of the airline, the destination, the time of takeoff.

All of that is real, confirmed. Did I buy the ticket for myself? Again, unless I have access to a credit card that I don't know about, I don't have the money to have bought a cheapo economy flight, let alone first class.

I could be imagining all of this, I say to Zia as I sit back and drink the terrible coffee that's now cold. I'm trying to be logical, practical. It's the least I can do under the circumstances. *I could have a totally separate email account and signed up for a credit card that I don't know about. Or I could be lying in a hospital bed right now with a mainline of drugs in my veins. Hallucinating all of this.*

Or, she says, *you could be in for the adventure of a lifetime.* She pauses. *Which one do you want it to be?*

Is it wrong the familiar excuse of being nuts feels like the right answer? *I'm scared,* I admit.

Of course, you are, she says. *They made sure you would be. But you're Anastasia Fenimore. I wish I could say we've been through worse.* She sighs. *Honestly, we haven't. I'd rather face swords and soldiers and near-death at his side than this endless frustration.* Zia's burbling joy returns. *It's not too late,* she says. *He's waiting.*

And if I decide not to go? I huddle in the plastic chair, staring at her through my own eyes in the glass like she's real.

Zia nods my head. *Then that's your choice,* she says. *This isn't my life to live. I'm already gone, Asta, only the remnants of me here to help you find what you're looking for. But I hope you remember.*

I don't understand, I say.

I know, she tells me. *It's a lot. I don't think I understand, either, to be honest. It has to be part of what brings us back every time. All I can tell you is we made him a promise a long time ago. A lot longer than you could ever imagine.* He said the same thing, that he promised "her" something, the woman he was looking for. Was he talking about Zia? About me? *We don't know how it's possible, only that it keeps happening. I don't have the right to ask you to make sure it's not the last time.* She's very sad now, retreating. *But I am asking. At least hear him out before you choose.* She laughs. *Sounds like he's coming for you regardless, so whatever happens, you're going to find out.*

That feels like failure. Why does that feel like failure? It has to be on me, damn it.

I send him a message to that same email. *See you soon.* Then I dump the bad coffee in the trash and go home.

Pack a small backpack. Call Janet for a day off.

And take a bus to the airport.

My new photo ID I had made to open a bank account is sufficient. My boarding pass seats me by the window in a pod I get to recline into. The flight attendant is sweet and offers me a warm hand towel that I use to press to my face, to soak away the terror I'm sure shows in my eyes.

What am I doing?

I turn down the offer of alcohol because the last thing I need is inebriation. I've spent my life behind a medicinal curtain, thank you. I do accept the offer of food, though, savoring the delicious chicken pasta and the chocolate brownie for dessert. Zia is quiet, still there in the back of my mind, but not speaking up and I don't address her, nor do I seek the distraction of the screen in front of me. I stare out the window instead at the fluffy clouds and do my best to remember.

She's not wrong about the frustration. I'm even

deeper in it by the time the plane lands a few hours later.

I have no idea what to do, I realize, when I disembark, nodding to the flight attendant, hesitating on the breezeway that leads to the gate. I follow the crowd to the exit, to baggage claim, surprised to find a tall, dark-suited man standing off to one side with a large, white sign that says, *Anastasia Fenimore.*

He takes my backpack when I approach him, leading me to a large, black car and seating me on the leather interior before closing the door behind me. And then we're driving, out of the airport and into the countryside, away from the signs to the city. I want to ask a million questions but there's a tinted plexiglass plate between me and him so I sit back and hold my own hands tightly in my lap while the unfamiliar landscape moves past my window.

The car slows at last, turning up a wide lane, a giant, metal gate swinging open to admit us. The low-key roll of my stomach turns to panic again, but I need to know.

What if I throw up in the bushes? I'm only half joking.

Better than on the front steps, Zia laughs. She's delighted, bright and light and full of energy. Happier than she's ever felt. Crazy or not, I'll take it. *You'll be fine. Trust me.*

For better or worse, not for the first time...

I do. Even if I'm really lying in a bed in a facility somewhere and this is all a dream.

Then it's safe to see it through, Zia says.

I'm here, aren't I? I wait for the driver to open the

door but only because Zia tells me to, hesitating now that we're parked in front of a huge stone mansion, a wide set of stairs leading to a massive front door flanked by pillars. *Sinking moment by moment into deeper delirium?*

The front door opens as I inhale the scent of fresh air, and I look up.

He's standing there. The man from the bar. The stranger with the beautiful eyes and the scent that holds sway over me. My heart sings a song I don't know but that fills me with so much joy I can't move.

El, Zia breathes. It's *her* joy, it has to be. And, for the first time since she's made herself known to me, she begins to weep.

"Anastasia," he says.

"Asta, my dear." He's not alone. Dr. Matt joins him, stepping out from behind him.

Slow-motion denial crushes me instantly. She's here. She can't be here. That means I'm in a hospital after all, that he's the delusion I feared he was and I'm about to wake up to the horror of the broken girl I was always told I am.

No. It can't be. Why is she…? Damn it. None of this is real after all.

And now I know for certain I'm doomed.

CHAPTER TWENTY-FIVE

Before despair can win, he turns to the psychiatrist with a deep frown.

"I'm very disappointed," he says. Like he sees her. Like he's the real one and she's not just emerging from my hallucination after all. "You weren't meant to interfere."

"And yet," she says as she gestures at me (she sees him too, she does, and that means he's real, right?) "you accept how easy it was to break this bond you claim to have."

He shakes his head while I try to figure out what the hell is going on, dread and panic and hope and many things I can't seem to wrangle argue and battle their way to dominance inside me. "She's here," he says. "Despite you." He sounds very satisfied by that, smiling at me. "As I always knew she would be." El's happy expression fades as he faces her again. "You may go, Tiamat." She doesn't move, staring him down. "Darken my door again, and there will be consequences."

What did he call her? Dr. Matt shrugs delicately at last, gracefully, walking past him and in my direction. She pauses next to me, looking into my eyes. Her amber ones fill with fire.

I'm not imagining it this time. I'm not pumped full of drugs so I think it's my imagination. They really do flicker with flame and, for a moment, the circle of her pupils turn to slits.

There's not much I can do but gape as she reaches out to touch my cheek with those horrific nails. I dodge her this time. I know better than to let her. "I only tried to help, my dear," she says. "To free you from this terrible, endless suffering." She glances just barely over her shoulder at the man who watches. "To do what was best for you."

I don't believe her for a second, not needing Zia's hiss of rage to prove it. An overwhelming need to punch this lying, deceitful and horrible woman in the face doesn't follow through, though my hands are shaking fists at my sides. "Don't touch me," I say. "Or come near me. Or speak to me ever again."

She exhales softly, climbing into the car I just exited without another word. I stand where I am and watch as the driver takes her away, down the long lane to the gate.

Before I finally turn and look up at him again.

He hasn't moved, the sorrow on his face returned. "I've missed you." His deep voice cracks but he shows no sign of embarrassment or attempt to correct the emotion he's shared.

"I wish I could remember." It seems like the right thing to say.

He nods, gestures for me to join him. "Elios Veles," he says, big hand pressing over his heart as he bows a little in my direction. So formal and yet so very much him it doesn't seem odd or awkward. I slowly climb to stand in front of him. When we first met (this time?), he'd only been on his feet for a moment. He'd been sitting down most of the conversation we'd had. I had no idea he was so tall, at least a foot above my 5'7". He feels massive standing there beside me, like he could engulf me in his arms and I'd disappear. But I'm not afraid of him, not afraid at all anymore.

"Hi, El," I say. I don't know what else to do.

He smiles, the brief flare of joy reaching his silver eyes with their flecks of gold. "Come inside, Anastasia," he says. "We have a lot to talk about."

His house is vast, the foyer massive in marble and polished wood but I barely notice it past the initial surprise, because he's next to me, his scent filling me with reminders that those things I thought weren't real, that were tied to trauma, had nothing to do with the lies Dr. Matt told me.

"Tiamat," I say. "Who is she?"

"She doesn't matter," he says gently to me as I

inhale the forest at night, chocolate and smoke. "She thought she was important, but that was her delusion." How interesting, his choice of words. "She never did matter, not really."

I want to touch him. The craving is so powerful I find myself sliding my hand into his. The ring on his finger is hot under my touch as he squeezes ever-so gently, tucking my hand deep inside his giant one. Everything about him is in balance from his wide shoulders to his narrow waist and hips, his long legs, his facial structure. But he's oversized, bigger than life, larger than truth and I find myself stumbling as I stare at him, trying to understand why he feels not quite normal while we walk.

Instead of watching my step. Not that it matters. The moment I trip, he's supporting me as if my feet didn't even touch the ground, and the burning inside me increases.

Only it's not the fire I'm used to, Zia's fire. It's something else, something hotter and more insistent and now I'm staring at his mouth.

Remembering what he tastes like. How do I remember what he tastes like?

I have to look away. I don't trust what I'll do if I don't.

Why does that make me want to giggle hysterically?

The bright light of the room we enter startles and distracts me. It's like he turned on a brilliant glow suddenly, and I'm looking around me with dazed wonder. It takes a moment for me to realize what I'm looking at, and when I do—

"It's me," I say, turning in a slow circle. Because it *is* me. Versions of me. In paintings and sculptures and photographs, filling the walls and pedestals and even covering the ceiling high above me, a massive portrait of me.

And him.

I should worry he's some kind of stalker, maybe? But who would choose to stalk someone like me?

He smiles at me again, the sorrow I remember gone from his face. "Not to call you vain," he says, "but you made sure we had a record of our time together in as many incarnations and as often as possible."

I did? "I still don't know what this is." Or do I? Because it's now as familiar as he is, though not for the reason he might think. The books I'm writing. The stories in my head. As I draw near to a portrait of the two of us, I know that blue dress I'm wearing, how my hair is piled just so in a cascade of curls while he stands above me in gorgeous blue velvet. I've seen that image before.

In my head. While I wrote down the outline for the sixth book in the series I'm still not so sure isn't a symptom of my insanity. My fantasy, Dr. Matt called it.

"How much *do* you remember?" He's standing right behind me and when I turn in surprise to look up at him, he's so close I could grasp the lapels of his jacket and pull him down to me if I wanted. I could taste his lips and find out if that memory of him is right.

What is wrong with me?

"I'm writing books," I blurt. Wave one hand around like an idiot. "About this."

He seems unsurprised by that, nods. "I feared you were right," he said. "But you still found a way to keep the memories despite your illness." El—not Elliot, *Elios*—looks up at the big painting on the ceiling. His tanned skin has an odd texture as his face contorts a little. Is that pain? No, grief. It's back and he's suffering and I have to make it stop. Which I do by taking his hand again. When he looks down, those gorgeous eyes are rimmed with tears. "You were so afraid at the end of your last life that you'd forget, Anastasia. I should have known you'd find a way to remember."

My last...

"You'd better tell me what's going on," I say, "before I do go nuts. For real this time."

He chuckles, leading me to a seat, a long, low sofa upholstered in a dark blue paisley. When he sits next to me, I almost regret it. Not because I don't want him there. To the contrary. I want him there *too* much. Now that I'm here, now that I've gone all in, there's no way this isn't ending in something heated and intimate.

How am I going to focus?

"Two thousand years ago," he says, "a young woman defied the dragon she and her companions had been sacrificed to. And on that night, I fell in love with her."

—fire, flame, the amber eye, a hand and a ring—

"Not a dream," I gasp that. So, I can focus after all.

He tilts his head. "Not a dream," El says. Turns and retrieves a book from the side table that he sets in my lap.

My book. *Dragon Girl.* I'm almost embarrassed when I meet his eyes again. "Not a dream," I repeat.

He smiles. "You embellished it a little," he says, free hand resting on the cover while the other gently cradles mine. "And we certainly didn't talk like that." His wry amusement has me giggling.

"Readers don't care about dialect," I say with a haughty air that really isn't like me at all, but I can't help it. "They just want the hot stuff."

Elios laughs, leaning closer. I don't think it's on purpose, with any intent, but it certainly makes parts of me wish parts of him weren't wearing a suit. Which has me blushing and trying to catch my breath while his smile fades to something that matches what I'm feeling.

"The rest," I gasp that. "I have to know."

He leans away again, as much as I wish he wouldn't. Elios' broad back presses into the sofa's low rise, silver eyes sad again. "We have no idea how you manage it," he says. "But since that first life you spent with me, you've somehow reincarnated yourself, over and over, never missing a chance. No matter how you passed, how long we had in each return, you always, always came home to me."

That makes no sense, of course, except that it's part of the series I'm writing so I just nod and accept.

How can I not? "What changed?"

He lifts my hand to his lips and presses them to my skin. The heat of his breath gives me shivers. But the kiss isn't passionate, it's soft and soulful and when he looks up again from that touch, he shrugs.

"Your last life ended with dementia," he says. "We knew you were dying long before you did. You recognized it, feared it. Not because you feared death. You never have." He touches my hair, my cheek, fleeting strokes with his big fingers, hot and tender, tentative. "At the very end, you didn't know me anymore."

I'm so sorry, I say in my mind. Not to him. Or to me. To Zia.

But she's not there. Where did she go this time? I almost panic, but he's still talking, and I focus on him.

"You *always* come back to me," he says. "Eighteen years later, twenty, sometimes a little more. Always you. Always remembering who you were and why you were back. But this time, you made me promise to do what you might not be able to. Just in case. That if you lost track of our life together, I'd find you."

My chest hurts and I find myself on the edge of sobbing. I'm almost thirty. All that time... "Where were you?" It's not fair and I don't know where it comes from, that accusation. That demand. And now I'm angry and it's unreasonable but it has to be Zia, doesn't it? What's left of her? Because I still don't remember, not really.

He takes the hit like he expected it. "You didn't come," he said. "I waited and you didn't come." Elios clears his throat. "I almost let you go." He shakes his head. "All this time." He repeats what I was thinking. "It may have been time, Anastasia. The Fates' means to let you rest at last."

The need to hit Dr. Matt is nothing compared to my desire to smack him. "You abandoned me," I choke. "You abandoned *her*."

He nods, not arguing or fighting the truth. "I thought it would be for the best," he says. "Except, I couldn't stay away. Not until I knew the truth." He releases my hand, spreading his wide. "I found you. But the worst had come to pass. Your fear. You didn't remember me." He doesn't reach for me again. "And it's all my fault."

CHAPTER TWENTY-SIX

I'm up and pacing because rage is awake and alive, and it wants me to lash out at him. Even though I know it's irrational to blame him for any of it.

"Tiamat," I say. Stop in my tracks and glare at him. Her accent. Now I know why it was familiar to me. He has the same one. Things click into place. "She's a…" I choke on the word he used.

"Dragon," he says.

Dragon. Right. "And you, what? Reincarnate like I do?" Two thousand years? I thought I had trouble with the "d" word.

"No," he says. "I'm always here."

"Some kind of vampire or something?" I'm being

flippant but he's not.

"Or something," he says. And waits for me to accept it.

Because I already know what he is.

"Dragons aren't *real.*" I fire that off at him like a weapon, hurtling it at him to hurt him. I've gone from intense attraction to flaming fury in a flash of rejecting any of this as truth or my life or anything but a delusion.

I need to wake up. There's a reason he feels familiar, I realize. I made him up. I made all of this up. If only I can believe the old line, the tried and true insanity plea. I can't though. It's barely hanging on by a thread. I've never felt so real in my life.

"Anastasia." When he says my name, it's a caress. "I thought I'd be alone forever. My kind are solitary. I spent millennia with only temporary companionship, as is our way." He doesn't rise or come closer physically, but he might as well be wrapping me up in his arms and drawing me against him the way his words seem to engulf me. It's the aching longing in his voice that catches me up, that strokes me like his fingers did just a few moments ago, though with more impact. "Until you."

I make a mental leap that has me very still. "Tiamat," I say. "Dr. Matt. You two…"

He nods. "We've had three eggs together," he says simply. "Two viable hatchlings. Only one made it to maturity. As is often the way of dragons."

"She's in love with you," I gasp at him. No wonder she did what she did. To keep us apart.

But he simply shakes his head. "We don't function in that manner," he says. "She doesn't understand love the way you do. The way you taught me to." Elios seems puzzled briefly, then sad again. "She's expressed her concern in the past. They all have."

"They?" *The other dragons, Asta*, my mind says. Not Zia. *Me.*

"My people have never understood what you and I have made," he says with gentle simplicity. "I fought it myself for a time. But you have never wavered, Anastasia. You have come back to me against every conflict, surpassed every confrontation, survived to land squarely at my side time and lifetime and age unending."

"Until now," I say. It still hurts, like betrayal.

"Until now," he says. "And yet, even now. Despite my failure."

I'm here because of him, though. And Zia.

Where *is* she?

"Dr. Matt," I say. "She was the dragon."

"That you were sacrificed to, yes," Elios says like it means nothing.

"Why did you save me?" I don't remember. The book I wrote never explained it, not really. Do I even know why?

He hesitates like it's an answer he's never been able to provide. "I heard you screaming," he said. "Defiant, not afraid." Funny, I don't recall it that way. "You were angry. Begged for the chance to prove yourself. And Tiamat was toying with you, as she often did with her prey," Elios looks away, out the window, gaze as lost as he is, in the past, no doubt. "I'd given up on that practice a long time before she did. Taken to walking among your kind. I wanted to understand your condition, the human experience. Such short lives, lived with such passion." He drapes one arm over the back of the sofa, lips pursing as he squints into history. "Perhaps you seemed an excellent subject to study, at first. I don't recall, I must admit. But there was something in you, Anastasia, a relentlessness, a steadfast demand to live, that I couldn't ignore." He turns his head, silver eyes sparkling. Real sparks, tiny ones, that make them glitter like the diamond in his ring. It only lasts a moment, but it's freaky and awesome at the same time and I'm again fighting the lure of him as he finishes. "From the moment we met, from the instant your voice drew me to you, I have been helpless to you."

"Is that why you didn't come looking for me?" He did, though. I have to remind myself of that. But too late, far too late. Again, not his fault, but blame falls regardless.

"Maybe," he says without hesitation or denial of responsibility. "Our lives have been intertwined for so long, I barely remember my life before you. You take up so much of what I am, Anastasia." He chuckles. "I was the one who wanted to understand humanity. So, in fact, the Fates themselves decided to give me what I asked for. Caution never crossed my mind."

Be careful what you wish for has never been so accurate.

"Tiamat," I say. "Dr. Matt. Why didn't she just kill

me?"

"She never understood you, either," he says. "I can only guess she and others like me wanted to fathom our connection. Or sever it, ultimately, if that failed. Whatever the case, they won't trouble you again." His jaw jumps. It's the only move he makes but I sense the anger in him despite the tiny motion. "No matter what happens here, I'll make sure of that."

He stands then, comes to me, long legs carrying him across the distance in two strides. Elios is suddenly in my space, leaning over me, both hands cupping my cheeks. My skin burns where he touches me, and I'm drowning in him, in his scent, in the depths of his crystal silver eyes with those dancing flecks of gold as he tilts his head.

"I won't blame you if you choose to leave," he says. "I have the means to erase what you now know, if you decide this is our last meeting." Elios hesitates, grief a flare of emotion before his face settles again, touch tender despite the heat of it. "Know that I love you," he whispers, hoarse and crackling. "As you taught me to love, Anastasia. Enough to let you go."

I don't want him to. That's the last thing on my mind. I want to throw my arms around his neck and kiss him, never, ever leave him again.

"I need to think about it," my traitor lips say. Why is logic winning now of all times?

"I wouldn't have it any other way," he says.

CHAPTER TWENTY-SEVEN

The hotel suite is opulent, to say the least, not at all what I'm prepared for, the giant king-sized bed canopied in the next room, the bathroom bigger than my apartment. Not that any of it matters. I pace the plush blue carpeting in the living area between two leather-clad white sofas, doing my best not to stop and stare at myself in the massive mirror that makes up the end wall.

I'm done judging myself. For now, at least.

There's a tiny part of me that needs reassurance, growing by the moment, and I finally take action because it won't be denied. Which means when I grab the very sharp knife from the tray of food that arrived for me without having to order anything, I'm shaking.

Blood wells at the tip of my finger when I stab myself. I stare at the deep, red drop and hiss at the pain I just caused, sucking the spot to stop the bleeding and tossing the knife aside.

Pinching myself feels irrelevant after that.

Either this is one hundred percent real or... I'm utterly lost. I can't decide which is worse. Or better, for that matter. I want to believe. My heart aches to trust. How can I just break over twenty years of conditioning, though? Pacing isn't helping, though it does burn up some of the energy that sizzles inside me.

Energy fed by fury that rises in waves I struggle to control.

If this is real, there are people in my life who have so much to answer for. My mother, for one. She knew I wasn't responsible for Dad's death. I can't make excuses for her. She had to have seen the final report, the pictures of my dragon in my room. A faulty pilot light on the stove is a far cry from accusing your own daughter of killing your husband and then condemning her to a lifetime of drugs, therapy and layers of guilt and despair.

All of which has horrible implications. Zia's question lingers in that surge of rage that demands accountability from Mom. *Where was your mother?* I don't know. I never asked.

Now I'm terrified of the answer. Because the only thing I can think of that might explain her absence and her accusations against me implicates her. Why else would she consign me to all those years masked by lies if she wasn't hiding something she had done?

I can't go there. I have no proof she was involved. For all I know, she really believes even now that I'm guilty. But the demand for answers won't be ignored and I realize I need to know more than just the history about who I am.

I want *all* the truths.

Then there's Dr. Matt. Fury against her is cleaner, sharper. It wobbles between embracing Elios' explanation, that she was once his mate, that she found me first and manipulated me to keep us apart after trying to eat me the first time around. The diabolical depth of her choice also has an excuse, though, if I'm buying into the entire insane explanation. She's not human. She's a dragon. They are immortal, limitless, endless. She doesn't think the way we do. Maybe she really did think she was helping me.

And, if she's not any of that, if she's just a psychiatrist, mortal human like me, she had her own reasons for wanting to keep me complacent. But I can't for the life of me figure out what those reasons might be.

That's the only thread that keeps pulling me back to believing Elios utterly. Why? What possible reason could Dr. Matt—the human doctor—have to lie to me about my trauma, to keep me drugged and pinned down and disoriented? Unless she's the batshit crazy one, which I suppose is entirely an option.

"I need to know," I whisper into the scented air of

the giant hotel suite. "I have to go home."

The thought of leaving him hits me so hard I have to stagger to the sofa and sit before I fall. One hand rises to cup over my heart that's pounding so fast I feel dizzy. *I've just found him again!* I hiss at that thought, drive it away. There's time to deal with this when I'm done with what could hold me back. Only then does the regret and anxiety retreat, leaving me burning still.

And determined.

My tablet hums. I reach for it, frowning at the message notification, surprised to find it's from Helen.

Asta, she writes in our social media thread, please come home. *I need to talk to you. I'm so worried about you.* Helen's worried about me? Janet must have told her I took a day off, but why would she worry?

I've already decided to go back, but even if I hadn't, her message would have made the choice for me.

I'll see you soon, I type and hit send. Before emailing Elios.

Hey, I wince at that opening but don't change it, *I have something I need to take care of.* I look up and into the mirror, meeting my own eyes before returning my attention to the screen. *It won't take long,* I add. *But I need a ride home.* I hesitate before I send the message. What if he tells me he's done? What if he rejects me? He doesn't owe me anything and me leaving again might trigger the end. Am I ready for that?

It's barely a minute before he responds.

Of course, he sends. There's a flight itinerary attached. He'd already bought me a ticket. Did he anticipate this? Does he want me to leave? The next line surprises as much as it soothes my fears. *I know you're perfectly capable, but do you want me to come with you?* I do. So very much. With an ache that begs me to say yes.

I can handle it, I send, furious with myself for turning him down. Except I really need to do this alone. Or I've been taught that asking for help ends badly every time.

Whatever, Asta.

His response is immediate. *Take all the time you need. And if you change your mind, just message me.* Relief is like his arms around me. I can feel him, smell him, taste him. Why can't I just say yes, please, come with me? *I'll be here when you're ready, no matter how long that takes. Even if it's the next lifetime.*

I exhale, sag. Send, *thank you.* Almost add, *I love you.* But I don't.

Even though I do. For better or worse, truth or delusion, I love him. I always have. Knowing he's waiting for me gives me more peace than he'll ever know. And the strength to do what I must. Time to face the past once and for all.

CHAPTER TWENTY-EIGHT

I'm in desperate need of a shower and a change of clothes by the time the car drops me at Helen's sister's house, but that can wait. Her messages have continued to devolve, my tablet's Wi-Fi blowing up as soon as I reach the airport.

You're in danger, she sent while I was still in the air, barely boarding the flight Elios put me on, returning via first class yet again in luxury I'm still processing. *Where are you, Asta? Please, you must come home.*

Some of her messages are gibberish, devolving into panic and despair, making no sense and as I scroll through the over twenty lines of text she sent to me, I'm beginning to panic myself. What is going on?

I take the steps to Janet's house two at a time, banging on the door though she has a doorbell,

Helen's terrified sister whipping it open and pulling me inside.

"She's had a breakdown," she whispers to me as she stops me in the entry. "Her psychiatrist is here."

Her... Helen doesn't have a psychiatrist. Dread is a dead weight inside me.

No. It can't be—

I step into the dimly lit living room and the first person I see is Dr. Matt. Helen huddles next to her, clearly medicated, the stoic and kindly woman I know and trust hunched and broken. When she looks up and meets my eyes, hers are filled with agony I know she's done her best to hide from the world, the loss of her daughter bare and exposed on her face.

Helen lurches to her feet and embraces me, clutching at me, making me her lifeline though I'm now barely hanging on myself.

As I glare at Dr. Matt who rises with a grace that shouldn't be possible.

Not for a human being.

"Helen, dear," the dragon Tiamat says in the guise of her fake caring, "it's going to be all right. Asta is here now."

"Asta, Asta," Helen murmurs my name, pulling away to touch my face with trembling fingers, tears trickling down her cheeks. She's pale, so pale, and her gaze is distant, her lips slack. Is this what I looked like when I was under the influence of the drugs Dr. Matt has given my friend? More than likely. There's a reason I could never look at myself in the mirror. I'm disgusted, but not by Helen. "Asta, you're safe, you're here." She exhales, but she's weeping, swaying. "Carrie," she says then. "I'm sorry, baby. I shouldn't have let you go."

She thinks I'm her daughter. And now I know the bitch has gone too fucking far.

I turn my body sideways, protecting Helen as best I can, knowing I failed to, ultimately. Determined to rectify that. "Let her go," I say.

"I'm afraid I don't know what you mean," Dr. Matt says, spreading her hands, those massive nails now talons to me. When I look at her, I no longer see the doctor I believed wanted to help me. All I see is the amber eye with the slitted pupil and fire. "Helen's condition is due to trauma, the death of her daughter. When she came to my office to see me, she broke down. A tragic reversal into unresolved issues that require medication—"

Lying. Bitch. "Let her go," I repeat through clenched teeth. "This isn't about her."

Janet looks back and forth between me and Dr. Matt, her horror and fear turning to anger. "What's going on?"

I hand Helen off to her sister with a firm frown. "Please take Helen into the kitchen," I say. "Dr. Matt and I are going to have a conversation."

Janet looks like she wants to argue, Helen still muttering my name. But she does as I ask, fear flashing over her face, and I wonder about the expression I wear that makes her afraid of me. It doesn't matter. One way or another, this ends now.

When I turn back, Dr. Matt has closed the distance

between us on silent feet, one hand outstretched. To touch me, no doubt. And now I know how she controls me.

How she's done all of it. Me, Helen's decline— There's one more person she's been in contact with who I really need to talk to, now. Though I'm positive that encounter is not going to end well. I need to focus on the here and now, however, on doing what I can to save the woman who saved me.

"Try it," I say, "and he'll never speak to you again."

Dr. Matt hesitates. "This isn't about your delusion," she says.

I bark a laugh. I can't help it. She's so predictable. "You disgust me," I say. I'm shaking but it's from rage and when she reaches for me again, I slap her hand away. That startles her, makes her back off a half step. I wonder if she's ever retreated from me before.

Victories, even small ones, are to be savored. And used to advantage.

"Let her go," I repeat that for the third time. "Whatever you have in mind, it's not going to work. I know who you are. I know what you did. You can try all you want, but you'll never control me again." I let that sink in. They're just words, but I mean every single one of them. "Either you come at me for real, admit what you did, who you are and why you chose to do it, or you back the hell *off*." She stares at me while I jab a finger in the middle of her chest. She's hot, her body almost steaming, faint wisps rising from inside her suit. The dragon surfacing. Let it. "But he knows, we both do. And your best wasn't good enough." That was ever so satisfying to say. "Nice try. Now, either kill me like you failed to the first time we met, or release her and leave me the fuck alone."

Dr. Matt—Tiamat—stares me down before she shrugs. "It was worth a try," she says. "I'll be seeing you again, Asta."

She leaves, just like that. I'm shocked that she gave up so quickly. Which means she has another plan in mind, and I need to be prepared. But before I can handle that, I need to deal with Helen.

Except, when I enter the kitchen, my friend is shivering, hugging her sister, and turning toward me, her eyes clear, her face shocked.

"Asta," Helen says. "What happened?"

If only I could tell her the truth. Hugging her is going to have to be enough.

CHAPTER TWENTY-NINE

Clyde answers the door when I knock. He's surprised to see me but not unhappy, letting me in almost immediately, though he's hesitant when I don't smile back at him or accept his offer to join them for dinner.

Jared doesn't look up. He knew I was coming. It's Mom I'm here for, whose terror passes over her face as I watch for the signs I know I'm going to see.

I don't wait for Mom to speak, tossing the file I printed off at the local post office onto the table in the middle of their dinner. "Just thought you'd like to review what happened the night Dad died," I say in a voice I don't recognize as my own. It's dull and heavy and angry all at the same time but I do nothing to temper it as Clyde shifts, concern on his face.

"Asta," he says, reaching for the folder. Mom's almost quicker but she's slowed by her fear and he takes it with an odd look for her when she tries to snatch it back. "What is this?"

I shrug. "The truth," I say. "Since I bet she told you the same thing she told me. That I killed my dad. Set the fire that ended his life." Clyde nods just a little, leafing through the news articles, stopping at the last page.

The official fire inspector's report that I requested from the city but had to turn to Jared to uncover. It helps to have a computer guy still feel guilty about betraying you, it turns out. The file that he sent to me just an hour ago is the last piece of this terrible puzzle that I'm putting to bed right now.

Mom just doesn't know it, yet.

"Asta," she says. "Pumpkin."

"Dad hated it when you called me that," I say. "And so do I. It always felt fake, Mom. Like you were trying too hard. I wonder why that is?" I point at the file in Clyde's hands. His eyes have widened and then narrow again, frown deepening as he reads before he looks up. But Mom's not looking at him.

She's staring at me with her mouth open, a soft, sad sound coming out.

"I need to know why you lied," I say. "Why you had me committed, Mom. Drugged me and told me I was broken." The rage sits below the surface but I don't call on it. I know it would consume me if I let it and I'm not going to give her that. I'm not giving her anything ever again.

Besides, I know why. At least, I know who. But Mom has to have her own reason for giving in to Dr. Matt's touch, her power. Like I did. Like Helen. Tiamat's real power comes from using the broken, sad and lonely parts of us against us. I'm as aware of that now as I am of my mother's hurt as she breaks down.

She falls more than sits, face in her hands as Clyde meets my eyes with his full of anxious fear.

"Asta," he says. Pauses and clears his throat. "Caroline, what is this?"

I half expect her to lie again. It's all she's done my whole life, after all. With or without Tiamat's influence to encourage her. But something in my mother has shattered—her turn—and when she inhales, she blurts truths I'm sure she never intended.

"He was leaving me," she cries, fists now rattling the dishes as she slams them down in front of her, the table shaking. Jared pushes back in surprise, scrambling to his feet, Clyde jerking a little. "You don't understand." Mom's faint wail follows as she rushes on, voice climbing in volume and pitch. "It was her idea! Dr. Matt. She convinced me you were damaged, broken. That you were a danger to yourself." She twitches faintly, a tic-like movement that starts in her hands and then travels up her arms to her head. It bobs twice before Mom speaks again, harsh whisper audible nonetheless. "It was in your best interest," she says, "to believe that you set the fire."

"In my best interest," I say, hearing the dull

flatness of my voice, feeling it. Feeding it.

"So you would heal," Mom says. "From the trauma of losing him."

I know this had nothing to do with Dad, at least, not from Tiamat's perspective. But that doesn't absolve my mother of what she did. What I know in my heart she did. To him and to me.

"From the trauma," I say, "of you killing him, you mean."

I know Clyde understands the implications of the paperwork he holds in his hands but he still gasps out loud at me saying it. Jared's surprise says he didn't know, either, even if he helped me to procure it. Whatever. I don't care what they think or feel. This isn't about them.

"He was going to leave me," Mom repeats, though quieter this time. "That night."

"We were going camping." I can see the gear in my mind, at the door. In the picture from the file.

"That's what he told you," she says. "But he closed our account that afternoon. The joint one. And removed me from his insurance policy." She doesn't look up, lips turning down into a semi-circle of sudden anger as hate—it's the only emotion I can call it— layers a kind of mask over her face that makes Clyde flinch again. "He was leaving me and he was taking you with him."

I just hold still and wait for the rest. It's not long in coming.

She stands abruptly, turning sideways, head down, not looking at any of us. But she can't hide the horror of what she did, the evil that drove her. Tiamat might have given her the nudge to finish the job, but it was all Mom and I have no illusions otherwise.

It's there, written all over her, as she speaks again. This time, her tone is as dull and empty as mine, like she's accepted it. Embraced it. And I accept at last she's to blame. Even as she confesses.

"You weren't supposed to be home," she says in a voice that I know, that's been manipulating her for as long as it manipulated me. "I knew if he left me, I'd have nothing. But the house was in my name. If it burned..."

"The insurance money," Clyde says, words thick. "Caroline."

She shrugs as though trying to shed his presence from the room. While I allow the pity that supplants the rage to win because this was Mom's fault but she likely wouldn't have gone so far on her own. She might have thought about it, but I despite everything, I can't bring myself to believe she'd have followed through. Not without help and encouragement.

I know who is really at fault. Even though my mother's bitterness was the wick on the candle, the dragon bitch was the flame. Tiamat has more to answer for than I realized. How old was I when she found me? I'd thought she'd come into this later than she did, but she was here all along. How much did it take for her to manipulate my mother into murdering my father so she could lay the blame on me and control me?

Diabolical. And very draconic, I guess.

"I needed the money to pay for a lawyer," Mom says. "To get custody of you." She finally looks up at me but my mother isn't there behind her eyes. Nothing is. Dr. Matt saw to that. The dragon has been using her far too long and now she's just a shell. "I needed to keep you safe." Dr. Matt's words fall from her lips. "From him."

Not Dad. This was never about my father. It was about me and me alone. Isolating me, keeping me from the continuation that I was meant to have. And now I want to kill that red demon more than anything. It's little comfort knowing that it's all real, but at least I'm finally there.

I leave, Mom sinking again to the seat at the table, Clyde staring at her in horror, Jared backing away from both of them. I've shattered the illusion, broken the seal of silence. The thing is, I really believe that Mom had it in her. Dr. Matt, Tiamat, just used what she found inside her to do what she needed to do. So while I feel for my mother—for the woman who gave birth to me, never my mother ever again—I know she did what she did because she chose to.

The cool evening air is a blessing when I stop at the street and stare up at the stars.

Freedom tastes like fresh air and for once, my heart is healed. I feel no pressure to fight, no goal to achieve. I've done what I intended to do. Any other tasks aren't mine.

That's a hard thing to accept. But if I go to El now, if I choose him because of Zia or Fate or whatever drives me to do so, am I not trading one control for another? I shudder when I lean into it.

Stubborn, Zia called me. And independent. Except those two labels used to be foreign to me. I've only found them recently. Am I willing to give up this freedom that I've finally earned?

The only truly frustrating part of it is realizing that, despite everything, Tiamat may have won after all. Because I still don't know what to do.

No. She had her reasons for wanting to keep us apart. Whatever those are, they aren't mine. I get to choose. Free will is a superpower I fall in love with as much as my heart yearns for El.

And until I decide, that's going to be enough.

CHAPTER THIRTY

I step back, Helen doing the honors, and smile as she cuts the ribbon in front of her with the embarrassingly big scissors I found for her online.

"Thank you to everyone who supported this effort," she says, squinting a little in the late summer sun as she gestures behind her at the big complex that she's just officially opened. "From the ache of grief and the ashes of loss, we rise stronger than ever." Her voice shakes a little but she's beaming. "And now, after six months and tireless work, The Carrie Shriver House for Women is now ready for our first of many residents and I couldn't be prouder of what we've done!"

I applaud right along with everyone else, overjoyed Helen named the new facility after her daughter, feeling a bit awkward and conspicuous from my place on the front steps. Janet's on my right side, holding my hand for support. The gathered media corral Helen, but I manage to avoid answering questions by ducking inside the foyer of the new complex, eagerly showing the first residents of the facility to their rooms.

Helen finally joins me, hugging me tight in the industrial kitchen with its gleaming stainless-steel counters and appliances, her recovery from Dr. Matt's attention long complete and her determination to see her dreams come to life again feeding her drive to make this happen.

"I don't know how you did it," she whispers in my ear as she squeezes me, "but thank you, Asta."

Did what? I flash her a bemused smile, shaking my head. "What do you mean?"

She frowns through her grin. "I didn't want to say anything before we opened," she says, "but that giant donation we received with your name on it made all of this happen." She pauses, tense as she touches my hand. "I thought you found some miracle doner."

Since I haven't yet contacted Elios, six long months passed worrying and wondering and trying to decide, it's clear he's not given up on me. Or the life I'm living without him.

In fact, I've talked myself out of messaging him a million times. I have a life here. I've built something of my own. My books are doing well, money no longer a problem, a nicer apartment and even a place with Helen if I want it luring me into normal and ordinary and a life of service that appeals to me very much.

After all, I don't really know him anymore. While it irks me when I think of it, was Tiamat right? This chance to break the cycle, to be free of the two thousand years I spent with him, feels like a real option. It's easy to set aside the past when I never got to live it in this lifetime.

To focus on a future that's only about me.

Helen's concern turns to irritation as she tugs on my hand. "What?"

I shake my head, smiling, forcing it but wanting it to be real. I won't ruin her opening day. "I'm glad the money came in handy."

She's frowning now. "You gave up something for me." That's not a question. "I've known it for months now. Something to do with that psychiatrist." She doesn't remember much of what Dr. Matt did to her and I'm glad. At least, when I've brought it up she's acted confused and has shrugged it off like it didn't happen. But it's clear to me now that she remembers more than she's admitted to. "Asta, tell me you're not here because of me."

I hesitate. Shrug. "I made my choice." I guess I did.

"I can't let you do that," she says and now she's crying. "Not after what happened to Carrie." Helen never talks about her daughter, especially now. "From the moment we met, I knew you weren't like the others, Asta. And you've been the kid I never got to love." She hugs me again, so tight I can't inhale but I don't care and now I'm crying, too. "Whatever it is you walked away from, I'll never forgive myself if you did it for me."

I don't get to argue with her. She releases me and hurries out, and I hear her voice as she talks with great enthusiasm to the women of the facility, sounding distant. As though she's put space between us.

Or I have. It's a weird, symbolic space that means nothing. I can follow her even now, go to the dining hall, to the large living room and hang out with the women who Helen has brought here to help heal and find a path where no path had been before.

But this isn't my place, I know now as I listen to her talk and lean back against the counter and cry a little more before sniffling and wiping my nose on a tissue.

No matter where I go and what I do from here, this part of my journey is over.

So, now what? I'm startled when Zia speaks up, though I shouldn't be. I've known all along she's still lurked in the back of my mind, waiting for me to make my choice. She sounds anxious but patient, and I sigh as I reply.

I don't know, I say. My heart clenches. *What do you want me to do?*

Well, that's a stupid question, she says.

I laugh. She's not wrong. *We could be done.*

We could, she tells me. *No one would blame you. It's been a long road, Asta. And not an easy one. Nor will it get easier, I think. If anything, she's only going to make things harder for us.*

Tiamat. *I'm positive of that. She's not done.*

Far from it, Zia snorts. *So, the question is, what price is worth paying for love?*

Two thousand more years? I can't even fathom it.

And two thousand after that, she says. *Or, we walk away. And this is the end of that story.*

Will I lose you, too? That's almost more painful to think about. My love for him is a distant ache, one I've learned to segregate, to live with like a fragment of me that will never be whole. But she's immediate, intimate, and we've been through so much together. I'm only now accepting that truth, that she's as much a part of me as she is important. Vital, even. The times she left me, she never really left.

If anything, I abandoned her. Can I do that again, knowing what I know as she confirms my fear?

Yes, she says without judgment or regret. *All of us.*

Wait, what does that mean? All of who? I tense, ready to ask, when she steps back, like a veil being pulled away from my mind—

And memories pour in. The past engulfs me like an ocean, voices and thoughts and history and emotions that were lost to me, behind the curtain of my last life—

She draws it closed again, leaving me gasping and out of breath. *You can be free,* she whispers. *It's a lot, Asta.* We're *a lot. But you can be less, if you choose to be.*

Or more. So much more.

I'm terrified. It's hard to admit.

Of course, she says. *Silly, we all were. Where's the fun, otherwise?*

I'm laughing. As I reach out and pull the curtain wide open. For me, not for him. Because I couldn't accept it otherwise.

Neither would he, Zia whispers. *Come, Asta. Come home to us.*

I take a breath. And dive into the ocean.

I don't pause when I climb out of the car, leaving my things behind for the driver to take care of. Elios stands at the top of the stairs and he's my only focus.

All I can think about. Since it all came back to me.

"We should go inside," I say as I breeze past him. I know what comes next.

Can't. Wait.

One eyebrow arches at me as he smiles, a lopsided tug of the corner of his mouth that is going to get him in so much trouble in about five minutes. "Make yourself at home," he says.

I turn and face him, hands on my hips, all cocky on the outside and quivering terrified on the inside. Still afraid, like I've always been afraid. Of him. For him. Because all it will take is one moment of hesitation from him and I'm going to crumble.

"That's what I'm here for," I say. And open my arms.

He steps into my embrace, ducking so I can slide them around his neck. How many times have I done this very thing? I'm off the ground, tucked against him, breathing him into me as I press my lips to his skin. The other half of me, the destiny I chose over and over.

I'm going to eat him alive.

"Anastasia," he says, voice low and vibrating as he just stands there. He is hesitating, but it's too late now. Too late to send me away. The fire that was lit is raging and nothing will put it out. Not even death. Never that.

And not even if I forget. Not ever again.

"Where have you been?" I push back and look in his eyes, like it wasn't my failing that put time and distance between us. That almost cost us what we've earned through years and love and sacrifice. "*So frustrating.*"

His laugh makes me shiver all over. "Now you know how I've felt for the last two thousand years."

I could try a wisecrack back because he's clearly earned one. Except he's kissing me, you see, and there's not a whole lot I can do when Elios kisses me.

Besides kiss him back. And that's just the beginning.

I wish he'd move faster as he carries me upstairs.

EPILOGUE

His skin is warm where I press my lips to his temple, glorious eyes closed, breathing steady in sleep. El has taken on the sheen of scales as he seems to do when he's resting, as though the real him sits just below the surface, ready for him to let the dragon out.

He's done so before, and I've loved every second of it.

At least, I think so. I slide out of bed, draping the silk robe he gifted me around my shoulders, tying it across my waist, the cool softness of it nothing like the hard heat of him. I almost go back to bed, but the breeze from the balcony lures me outside to the table overlooking the garden and my laptop resting there.

I've lost so much, my body aching with the need to remember every single moment. Yes, with the veil pulled back and my return to my lives, I've recovered much of who I was. But not all. Physical contact has helped further remind me, intimacy awakening more.

So did the hours we spent talking, laughing. El's deep voice telling me stories I clutched at like a desperate child looking for more, always more. I think we'll spend the rest of this life trying and never satisfying my need for all of it.

Because it's clear to me that while I've forgotten, Elios remembers every single moment in perfect clarity. And the pain of my loss is only mitigated by the joy he has in telling it all to me again like it's the first time.

It's the first time for me.

Not for all of it, no. But there's so much I still can't hang onto for longer than instances of reckoning and I know that despite the Fate that brought us back together, I can't risk losing him again.

I *will not.*

He might not know it, but he was made for me and me alone. I smile down at the glowing screen in front of me. An all-powerful dragon Helios, known as Ra, Apollo, and so many more names that history has forgotten, immortal and nearly invincible, he has no hope against me. Or the love that I feel for him, the love I kindled in him that he never knew before we met.

It's the secret, you see. To how I keep coming back. I might not remember everything, but I remember that. A pact I made with myself to never let him go. Anastasia, Asta, Zia, every life, every time. I don't need magic. I just need love.

And Elios.

But this human body is fragile though his dragon one is not and there will come a time again when I leave him. Giving Tiamat the chance to come between us as she has done so many times before. Which means there's also a chance to forget him again or lose him because of her. I simply can't have that. I have far too much invested in us both to let anyone come between us.

Not the bitch of a dragon queen. And not even me.

I have no idea what the Fates have in store. Why my love has won their approval and this endless reincarnation to be with him. Or what's coming for us in the future. Deluded or not, in the cool welcome of the fragrant breeze that reminds me of the deep, dark forest, rich chocolate and smoke from a thousand fires, I open a new document.

And begin to type. Our stories.

So I'll never forget. Ever again.

AUTHOR NOTES

My darling reader:

As many of you know, I hear voices. And I've lived with depression and anxiety since childhood. Asta, however, is not me. As much as I'd love a dragon of my very own, Elios belongs to her and I have no illusions about love or romance or even magic.

As sad as that makes me sometimes.

Still, when she came to me—when they both did, as is rarely the case—I couldn't say no. This book is far outside my normal wheelhouse. I write about love, yes, but peripheral to other things. And I've avoided darkness in the last ten years or so, aside from a few exceptions. Even my murder mysteries have a happier, lighter humor to them.

It wasn't hard to write this book, though. Asta held my hand through the whole thing. Nor did it go the way I thought it would. That being said, there are more stories to tell in so many genres from so many lifetimes they spent together my mind boggles. They agreed to give me some time to work on other projects in between, but I have a feeling their next book—their first story—*The Sacrificial Heart*, will be coming along sooner rather than later.

That being said, I hope you enjoyed meeting Asta, Elios and the terrible, troubling Tiamat.

As always, stay safe and healthy out there and be as good to one another as you can.

Best, Patti

ABOUT THE AUTHOR

EVERYTHING YOU NEED TO know about me is in this one statement: I've wanted to be a writer since I was a little girl, and now I'm doing it. How cool is that, being able to follow your dream and make it reality? I've tried everything from university to college, graduating the second with a journalism diploma (I sucked at telling real stories), am an enthusiastic improv performer (if you've never tried it, I highly recommend making things up as you go along as often as possible) and I get to teach and perform with an amazing group of women I adore. I've even been in a Celtic girl band (some of our stuff is on YouTube!) and was an independent filmmaker (go check out the Lovely Witches Club). My life has been one creative thing after another—all leading me here, to writing books for a living.

Now with multiple series in happy publication, I live on beautiful and magical Prince Edward Island (I know you've heard of Anne of Green Gables) with my multitude of pets.

I love-love-love hearing from you! You can reach me (and I promise you, I'll always message back) at patti@pattilarsen.com. And if you're eager for your next dose of Patti Larsen books (usually about one release a month) come join my mailing list! All the best up and coming, giveaways, contests and, of course, my observations on the world (aren't you just dying to know what I think about everything?) all in one place:

http://bit.ly/PattiLarsenEmail.

Last—but not least!—I hope you enjoyed what you read! Your happiness is my happiness. And I'd love to hear just what you thought. A review where you found this book would mean the world to me—reviews feed writers more than you will ever know. So, loved it (or not so much), your honest review would make my day. Thank you!